More Critical Praise for *Manhattan Loverboy:*

"Part Lewis Carroll, part Franz Kafka, Nersesian takes us down a maze of false leads and dead ends . . . told with wit and compassion, drawing the reader into a world of paranoia and coincidence while illuminating questions of free will and destiny. Highly recommended."
—*Library Journal*

"A tawdry and fantastic tale . . . Nersesian renders Gotham's unique cocktail of wealth, poverty, crime, glamour, and brutality spectacularly. This book is full of lies, and the author makes deception seem like the subtext of modern life, or at least America's real pastime . . . Love, hate, and falsehood commingle. But in the end, it is [protagonist] Joey's search for his own identity that makes this book a winner."
—*Rain Taxi Review of Books*

"The dark recesses of the modern mind provide the backdrop of Nersesian's hilarious and warped passion play, *Manhattan Loverboy* . . . the dense story surges with survivalist instinct, capturing everyman's quest for a sense of individuality."
—*Smug Magazine*

"*MLB* sits somewhere between Kafka, DeLillo, and Lovecraft—a terribly frightening, funny, and all too possible place."
—*Literary Review of Canada*

"Nersesian's literary progress between *The Fuck-Up* and *Manhattan Loverboy* is like Beckett's between *Happy Days* and *Not I. The Fuck-Up,* though odd, is more accessible and easily enjoyable; *Manhattan Loverboy* is better . . . *MLB* is about how distance from power and decision-making can skew our reality, can leave us feeling like pawns in an incomprehensible game."
—*The Toronto Star*

"Nersesian's easy command of comic imagery is a reader's joy."
—*Punk Planet*

Also by Arthur Nersesian

The Fuck-Up
Akashic Books, 1997
MTV Books, 1999

Suicide Casanova
Akashic Books, 2002
(trade paperback edition forthcoming in 2005)

Unlubricated
HarperCollins, 2004

Chinese Takeout
HarperCollins, 2003

dogrun,
MTV Books, 2000

East Village Tetralogy
Bookstreet, 1995
(four plays, soon to be reissued
by Akashic Books)

Tremors & Faultlines:
Photopoems of San Francisco
Portable Press, 1995
(poems)

New York Complaints
Portable Press, 1993
(poems)

Tompkins Square & Other Ill-Fated Riots
Portable Press, 1990
(poems)

Manhattan Loverboy

Arthur Nersesian

Akashic Books
New York

Published by Akashic Books
©2000 Arthur Nersesian

Design and layout by Fritz Michaud
Cover photo by Sasha Kahn
Chapter illustrations by Elizabeth Elliott
Title page illustration by Kim Kowalski
Author photo by Delphi Basilicato

ISBN: 1-888451-09-2
Library of Congress Catalog Card Number: 99-96428
All rights reserved
Printed in Canada
Third printing

Akashic Books
PO Box 1456
New York, NY 10009
Akashic7@aol.com
www.akashicbooks.com

Portions of this book have appeared in the *Portable Lower East
Side* and *Big Wednesday*.

*To Burke Nersesian
and Patricia Gough*

Thanks to:

Paul Rickert
Don Kennison
Mike McGonigal
Alfredo Villanueva
Nathan Henninger
Alexis Sottile
Johanna Ingalls

"Did you make love with her?"

[Legal proofreading is the closest I've ever come to being submerged in a sensory-deprivation tank. Forty-one hours in a law-office cubicle, proofing a mark [the new document] against a master [the original, revised document], slugging line to line, is a task that, despite the technical terms, requires all the intelligence of a fast-food cashier; the less brainpower you have the better. It was in the throes of the final arch-seconds of the tip-top hours of a forty-one-hour shift—forty-one chain-smoked, coffee-bleached, fluorescently-blinded, street-noise-obliterated, air-conditioned, deli-sandwiched hours of proofreading in the Nietzschean heights of one of those thunderously towering office buildings [the shadow of which obscures us all] in the Wall Street section [an area so dense with skyscrapers that if you could open the window of one and reach out, you'd grab a fistful of steel and glass from another building [but since the whole hundred-plus stories of the fucking building is a single, never-ending metal window pane—one of those buildings alone could make you hunger for the nuclear annihilation of mankind and all its loathsome symbols—that you can't open anyhow, let's not even discuss it!]]—that I fell in love [a/k/a. a.p.].]

CHAPTER ONE

LA VÍA DEL TREN
SUBTERRÁNEO
ES PELIGROSA

Long before love there was solitude. Solitude begat need. Need begat anguish, and anguish brought me to love. Before I was a proofreader, I was a solitary graduate student. Many years before I was a student, I was an orphan. A very tall and silent lady from the Bundles O' Joy Adoption Agency escorted me to my new home. My adopted father thanked her, led me into his study, and carefully explained his motives for having me brought there.

"We'll try to love you, Joey, but we should explain that you're something of a substitute."

"A substitute?" I uttered, barely able to pronounce the word.

"Mrs. Ngm." That was what he called mother. "She's not like other women." At this point, my new-found mother emerged.

"Sir?"

"She's barren." He pointed to her lower reaches.

"And Mr. Ngm," Mrs. Ngm put in, "he's…inadequate."

"What does that mean?"

Mrs. Ngm went to the fruit bowl and tore open a tangerine.

"Do you see any seeds in this tangerine?"

"No."

"This tangerine is Mr. Ngm."

11

Their sense of inadequacy was passed on to me. They treated me very well, but not like parents. And they never failed to explain that I was only someone picked at random to fill an irrational parenting urge. Yet even this parental urge was not very apparent. Mr. Ngm rarely came home after that day, and Mrs. Ngm kept dashing out of rooms as I entered them.

I'm not sure whether this is a syndrome for adopted children, or whether it was just my own reaction to adoptive non-parents, but as I grew older I became increasingly obsessed with the identity of my real parents. This obsession, unfulfilled, eventually manifested itself in an acute interest in histories.

Faulkner said that American Indians said that the spirits of their ancestors said something like, man can't own the earth because the earth owns man. Man's identity is suited to his parcel of earth. We are but a single cell in these long bloodlines of countries and cultures. People are the living earth, they are the terrain come alive: Arabs are the desert, unchanging yet turbulent; the English are the sea, humid and unfathomable; Russians, in a variety of ways, just go on and on; Americans are the youngest sons of the earth and act immature. But the American melting pot of integration isn't even hot yet. The twentieth century was the century of immigrants; we can still see our torn roots elsewhere.

I clearly remember the day my preschool teacher asked what everyone's heritage was. Young as they were, my classmates bleated out: "I'm Irish," "I'm Afro-American," "I'm Vietnamese," etc.

But I, little Joseph, was left dumb. I was the rootless orphan. As I got older, I spent more and more time in dark, deserted libraries, searching through history books for my face, my race. Though I never found myself within the photos or descriptions of these worldly books, this compulsion eventually left me with a vast knowledge of history.

Ignorant of history, you think that the world starts when

you're born and ends when you kick. But me, I'm thousands of years old. I've survived wars, revolutions, intrigues, and catastrophes of all varieties. I can tell you intimate details of Pharaohs and Cataracts from both the Upper and Lower Nile, from Higher and Lower Civilization. I can give excruciating descriptions on how to get from one administrative building to another in early Byzantine Constantinople. I read, studied, became buddies with personalities on fire and confidantes of God. If I were to see William of Orange, or Roman Emperor Marcus Aurelius (who strangely resembled long-retired, New York TV community-chronicler Chauncey Howell), or any number of ancient potentates on the street, I'd be able to stop them and ask what they were doing alive in New York.

* * *

I arrived too late for the dorm-room lottery during that first semester at Columbia. But I was intent on not missing an academic year. When I informed Mr. Ngm of the situation, he sent a memo explaining that my scholastic budget was pre-fixed. Life beyond that would be a test of self-reliance.

I searched the ads in the papers and fliers in laundromats. With a limited amount of money, and not picky, I finally narrowed it down to a choice between a cozy studio in Williamsburg, Brooklyn (one hour away from school), or a wide stairway in an upper West Side loft (a mere ten minutes away).

The stairway was a discontinued passage in a large loft building. The landlord, I learned, would have demolished the conduit, but there was a possibility that the upper floors in the loft could be turned into commercial space. If this occurred, the owner would need the stairs to comply with building codes; so he left it intact.

The place was currently residential; so he renovated the stairway and advertised it as a "mini-triplex-studio." It wasn't as bad as it sounded. Like the body itself, the top landing of this stairway/apartment contained a nutritional gateway, my kitchen, the second landing a cushion of fat, my bedroom (my bed was a 4' x 3' piece of styrofoam—I had to sleep curled like a cat), and the final landing, the bathroom and exit.

In life, we are born and we slip from day to day until we die. Although there are signifying days and stages of life, there is no clear moment when we might say that we had only practiced living until now, and henceforth we shall actually live. After three undergrad years in that stairway studio, I realized that it was time to reach a landing, a new start. I decided to circumcise my adopted-family name. I planned to give myself a name with a national heritage that more closely resembled where I believed I came from, though where exactly that was was still a riddle to me. Realizing that I might never be absolutely sure, I felt I might as well give my allegiance to a culture worthy of my respect.

But were there any? Of all the great cultures that had ever flourished, of all the imperial civilizations, not a single one had stood the test of time. Their glory had faded. All that remained were crass, consumer societies, mere islands for corporate empires to bridge and tunnel.

One night around this time, I was wandering around the exasperating East Village feeling depressed in the French tradition. I clearly remember a boy in his late teens hidden under a huge, floppy fedora and clad in a baggy, out-of-date suit, who rushed up and asked me if I were Jewish. I thought about it, and decided to play a hunch.

"Yes."

He hustled me off into an unwashed Winnebago and said it was time to reaffirm my faith. Together, we submerged into a Mitzvah tank. He asked my name. He asked again.

"Levi," said I, thinking more of the jeans than the genes. Rolling up my sleeve, he wrapped a leather thong around my arm and led me through an ancient chant. I mumbled, faking the words. I wanted, needed the cleansing. His chanting beckoned Hollywood trailers of ancient epics: Charlton Heston in robes and beard, Peter O'Toole in *Masada*, Richard

Gere in *King David*. I saw the diaspora pass before me, and looking upon those wandering and beleaguered people, my eyes filled with tears. I saw myself in that sandswept caravan, my people, my past. Suddenly, out of nowhere, a large-headed, red-haired, red-faced Hasid appeared, and with a single sniff he started shrieking.

"Dos is a goy, a goy! Out with him!"

Even after being thrown out of the van and screamed at in public, I didn't give up the faith. There were little things, odd signs, that revealed to me my kinship with the thirteen great tribes. I craved gefilte fish, matzoh, and sickly sweet wines. Flatchki (tripe) and platski (potato pancakes) were delicious, and knishes were always a treat. Saturdays were a kind of natural sabbath. And I adored the tumbling sounds—*scholum*, *yehuda*, and *menachem*—like big drums rolling down a stairwell. Soon, I found myself wandering in this great Jewish mist, a hazy history that unfolded forever backward.

I knew a lot of baggage came with being a Jew, but I was good at carrying bags. I kept my Mitzvah name, Levi. I let my sideburns grow long and began to train myself. With most of my core courses complete, I switched my minor from philosophy to Hebrew and began studying the ancient laws and customs.

In the student dining room, there was a row of tables where Israeli exchange students sat. Without their permission, and although I didn't live on campus, I joined my happy friends. I tried to speak about historical and political matters with them. They were polite, but they seemed a little bewildered by me. They seemed suspicious.

I got a job that January at a kosher pizza place. It was my last semester before graduation, and I wanted to make enough money to visit the Holy Land. I wrote the parents that the two hundred fifty-eight steps of the stairway studio was too much of a test. I couldn't hack it. From New York, I made preparations to join a kibbutz. After getting my BA, but just before departing, I sent out applications to several elite and exciting graduate programs. No sooner were they mailed, though, then I realized that my life was on a new and different course— Israel.

* * *

As I stepped off the plane, I felt it. As sure as Little Joe was from the Ponderosa, I was a citizen here. The kibbutz was fun. I was brought into the fold. With my fellow man and woman, I planted seeds and harvested the crops. Afterwards, I sat around overly-laden tables until late at night, exchanging tales, folk dancing, or weeping to sad, quickly translated songs of the motherland. I was one of them, only perhaps I did behave a little differently, a little strangely. For some reason, as if I had an acute case of Tourette's Syndrome, I couldn't stop ending every sentence with verbal ejaculations like: "And may I die killing the vile invader of our blessed soil!" Perhaps I was a little over-zealous, trying to compensate for being a convert. (But I'm not sure that merited the nickname "Goy Boy.")

Despite that, though, I was having a good time, really enjoying myself. The problem was that this wasn't the way it was supposed to be—it wasn't supposed to be fun. I was expecting a more spiritual thing.

I left the kibbutz after a month and moved to the Holy City, Jerusalem. There, I devoted myself to the reading of holy books and religious training. I got heavily into chanting and wailing. Whatever it was I was expecting, I was certain it was close at hand.

One day, while davening at the base of the Wailing Wall, I smote myself on the chest. It made a hollow sound. I did it again, and then again and again, harder each time, until everyone around me quit wailing and moved away. I didn't pay attention to them—I was on to something.

What was that sound? It was something important, I

knew that. But what? Then it all became clear. It was an absence of identity. It was the great gap in my soul that could never be filled.

I wrote a letter to the Bundles O'Joy adoption agency demanding the name of my true parents. A month later, I received three letters. One was from the adoption agency saying that it was protected information and referring me to the legal department of some large company. Another letter was from my adoptive parents. The last letter informed me that I had been accepted into a strange and wonderful graduate program. The fact that all of these letters arrived at once struck me as a divine sign.

The Ngms informed me that they were worried about my aberrant behavior and, if I chose to return immediately, I wouldn't have to live in a stairwell. An uncle whom I had never even known had just died, and I was eligible to take over the title of his huge, inexpensive Manhattan apartment in the Silk Stocking district of the Upper East Side. It seemed as good a time to leave as any. So I returned to Gotham City. At a corner diner in Gramercy Park, I met Mrs. Ngm. Or at least she said she was Mrs. Ngm.

"Mrs. Ngm, you look quite different from how I remember you."

"This is what a lifetime of housework does to a woman's body."

"But you look younger, better than I remember."

"Housework is a good thing," she replied. I was given a form to sign, a set of door keys, the address to the new place, and the blessings of Mr. Ngm. She informed me that some of his brother's personal effects still littered the place. If I wanted to, I could throw them out.

"Where is Mr. Ngm?" I asked adoptive Mama.

"The business is going under," she nodded sadly. Adoptive Dad, who was almost always at work, made a career of trying to save his dying Bonsai plant business.

"Say hi to him for me."

She bowed low, smiled brightly, turned to go, but stopped suddenly and added, "Mr. Ngm asked me to inform you that you are the trustee of his heart." If only I had an organ donor card.

I thanked her and headed to my new homeland. The apartment was a pin cushion to my needling spiritual disappointment. It was cheap, and I was assured it was spacious. But I expected little as I dragged my bags up the stairs of the large tenement. When I threw open the door I gasped a bit. It was the only time in my life that something had surpassed my expectations in a positive way.

The apartment was huge and wide-open like a great indoor meadow, an entire floor with a cathedral-high, pressed-copper ceiling. A small bathroom and kitchen were partitioned off to the rear. Windows in the front lined the avenue. In the back, however, the windows were built on a courtyard that was so narrow I'd have to go on a diet if I ever contemplated suicide by jumping through them. They looked out to windows of a new condominium that was built just inches away. I kept the window shades pulled for privacy, but no matter what time it was, day or night, I'd always hear a party through those windows.

My dead uncle had lived in one quarter of the huge hall, away from the street. The other three-quarters of the place were empty and thick with dust. That lived-in quarter of the apartment was cluttered with old, broken furniture and strange, classical garbage that he had accumulated over the years. Statues, friezes, birdbaths, archways, and an apparent sarcophagus, among other things, cluttered the rear quarter of the place. There were also boxes of yellowing pop psychology books and science fiction novels.

While taking a dump one morning, I noticed that the toilet wasn't fastened to the floor—it could be lifted up and swung sideways. With a little maneuvering, I discovered a hiding place had been created by my adoptive father's furtive brother. Inside the lost lacunae was an old New York City Subway map.

Israel had been good to me, but it didn't bring resolution. After returning to New York, I realized late one night what I had to do. I had my name legally changed to cold vowels. Not since Travolta donned a three-piece polyester had there been such a significant statement. It's bad enough that most given names are silly clichés decided by giddy, post-adolescent parents flipping through baby-naming books, but a surname should be more than a bland, culturally assimilating moniker. A name should be a unique definition of the man himself. In New York, I found myself: I was a man without a consonant—Joey A-e-i-o-u.

* * *

The B. Whitlock Memorial Fellowship for Academic Achievement in History had a ring to it. Even though it was offered at Columbia, I'd never heard of it. In fact, I never found out how I got this covert, coveted Fellowship. I'd never recalled applying for it. In my registration packet, I was informed that it was automatically bestowed on the undergraduate who showed the highest distinction in history. The year before, the preceding Whitlock scholar had dropped out, and I could find out nothing about him. So I was the only student in the program. The prerequisites were equally mind-boggling. It required course work that jumped departments and even campuses. The best description I had of it was given to me by its director, Professor Flesh: "This program qualifies you to lead a once prosperous nation in economic decline back into its glorious, halcyon days." It was better than working in an office.

With my apartment taken care of, and tuition covered, I only needed pocket money, so I went out and got a part-time job where every intelligent, self-hating person works—a bookstore, in particular the Strand Bookstore.

On weekends, I'd putz around doing shit work. By week-days, I played the role of the esteemed Whitlock scholar. Much of that role consisted of evening tête-à-têtes with tee-totaling professors who assigned difficult-to-find books, often lent to me off their own shelves. Exams were oral. Papers were only accepted if they were published in one of sixteen academic publications in fields related to the course. It was a challenge at first. Somewhere in the back of my mind, I still had faith that through knowledge all answers could be reached. I would learn or stumble upon some clue of nothing short of my very identity. But after an adolescence of reading histories, and then another year of this program, moving minutely across the same old ground, I started losing it. I wanted to join the ranks of the petite bourgeoisie. A thankless, hands-on job, like firefighting was just the thing. By the final semester of the program, I actually considered dropping out and taking the civil service test. But before my decision was solidified, something odious happened.

On an overcast day, more than a million years ago, at the start of my ice age—it was the final term in the program—I was called into Professor Flesh's office. He said, "Reaganomics are still the gladiator games of our age."

"Huh?"

"That's how historians will see this."

"What?"

"The rich have made a contest out of cuts; the lower tiers are again in the cold. I'm sorry, young Josef, call it Reaga-mortis."

He informed me that my award, the Whitlock Memorial Fellowship, which had sustained me through a year and a half in the costly program, had, without rhyme or reason, been rescinded. Unless I could find some other way of financing myself, I was out of the ball game.

"This is my last term!" I appealed. "All I have to do is hand in my thesis, and then I'll get a quick appointment in some

Catholic girls college in some economically depressed area, and I'm set for life."

"Sorry, Joey, but it's out of my hands."

"Who cancelled my award? Why? I was good."

"Only the Lord and perhaps Dean Sovereign can say."

"Dean Sovereign? Where is he?"

"In Low." Low, the building behind the seated statuess, has the biggest front stoop anywhere. Up I went and in through the halls that Mark Rudd, student activist and campus leader of the S.D.S., had seized over twenty years ago.

"Halt!" groaned a security guard. I explained that I was trying to find out who had left me out in the cold, and that I was hoping Sovereign could assist. The security guard asked to see my ID. I showed it to him. He asked if I had an appointment. No. He pointed toward the door and said, "Out."

I asked to see his superior. A button-bursting, seamstressing sergeant informed me that Sovereign only saw celebrities, the filthy rich, or, at the very least, people with appointments. Proper channels had to be observed. As he walked me out past the Alma Mater statue, he said, "Try calling first."

I raced to the nearest pay phone and called. A secretary answered, "Dean's office. Can I help you?"

"May I ask your name, dear?"

"Veronica," she replied, "Why?"

"Hi, Veronica," I started, and then, releasing the hostility slated for the security guard: "I'm trying to find out what motherfucking organization is behind the severing of my fellowship. Now you could tell me, Veronica, or I could go through the Freedom of Information Act and sue the shit out of this cocksucking university, *capisce*?"

After a gasp, she laughed.

"Oh, you think this is funny?"

"What is your fellowship?"

"What are you going to do? Tell me that I can only find out

that sort of information through the mail? Fuck that! I have my rights! What's your nationality?"

"Calm down," she replied, "What program are you in?"

"Fine, we'll go through this little farce, this charade. My name is Joseph Aeiou and I'm..."

"Aeillo..."

"No, Aeiou, and I'm in the contemporary..."

"How-'r-ya?"

"No, Joseph Aeiou, in the masters program in hist..."

"Yagoda??" she asked.

"No, asshole, Aeiou, like the fucking vowels, A-E-I-O-U! Got it?"

"Put a cap on the foul language. I'm trying to help you."

"Spell it back to me, just to assure me you got it." She did.

"Good, now this was my last semester, see..."

"What was the program?"

"I was in the division of contemporary history. And all I had to do was hand in my butt-fucking thesis, and some fascist..."

"One second," she said, but I had already given her too many seconds; I just kept talking: "Some fascist elitist organization cuts me and laughs it off, lady...." She came back on the line.

"Hello, Joseph."

"...What you're doing is ripping my nuts off, veins, arteries, and all. Do you want to do that, lady? Do you really want to know what's inside those soft little sacs, lady? Do you want my oozy balls on your conscience?" Although she couldn't see it, I grabbed my nuts to bring the point home.

"Have them messengered in," she giggled.

"You're pushing it, lady!"

She was laughing at my expense! "All right, I'm really not supposed to give out this information."

"Please, I swear I won't tell that you're the one who betrayed them."

"Say please."

"Please," I said.

"Say, 'I'm sorry for being such a gutless asshole, but I'm just a scared little faggot.'"

I couldn't believe she was asking such a thing, but what could I do? I was too beaten down for any pride. I repeated what she'd told me to say.

"All right," she said very matter-of-factly. "Mr. Andrew Whitlock, fifty-three years old, is your benefactor. He made the decision to cut the award."

"Very shrewd!" I complimented her on her cruel tact.

"What are you talking about?"

"Trying to give me the brush-off with just the name. What's a name? I can't do shit with a name. You must think I'm abysmally stupid. You must hate me with a personal vengeance. What country are your people from?"

"Do you have a pen or pencil?"

"Don't give me that false concern, bogus-hospitality shit! You despise me just as much as I despise you."

She hung up the phone on me. I called her back. "Please don't hang up. I'm sorry."

"I hear street noises in the background. Are you calling from a pay phone?" she asked.

"Yeah," I replied, "and my quarter's going to run out soon, so please just give me the number."

"I'll give you his business address if you yell at the top of your lungs, 'I'm a fucking asshole!'"

"Haven't you scarred me enough?" I appealed. She hung up.

I called her back. She said hello, and I yelled, "I'M A FUCKING ASSHOLE! Now give me the fucking number." She read me a business number.

"Have a good day, sir."

"If I ever see you, I'll scoop your ovaries out." I hung up the phone on the bitch.

Cutting a young man's grant money was like fooling with his inalienable rights or the reagan between his legs. No one fools with my inalienable Jeffersonian rights—or my reagan. America had survived nine wars—not including Panama, the Gulf, and a combative catering task (Somalia)—all so I could go to school. I dialed this Whitlock's business number. A secretary answered.

"Where the fuck is your office? I'm gonna Unibomb your Somali warlord and toss his body parts into Jeff Dahmer's cage..."

She hung up on me. I called her back about eleven minutes later and, pinching my nose to achieve a nasal falsetto, told her that I was a bike messenger. In order for them to get a very valuable tubular document, I needed to know the firm's location. She gave me a Wall Street address.

Stepping off the train at the Wall Street stop, I knew I was entering very dangerous territory: an office building during business hours.

As I walked into the militarized zone, I realized that my only chance was to get him out in the open, away from the other suits. I located a vast rhombus of a building loaded with security and elevators. The dynastic firm was Whitlock Incorporated, and I later learned that Whitlock was the last of his inbred line. Like the plot of some low-budget horror film, he had to reproduce or, after two hundred years, the name of the firm would change.

I took the elevator up, swallowing a couple of times to relieve the ear pressure as the altitude increased. Where were they when you needed them: feces-flinging rocker G.G. Allin, mad bomber George Metesky, still-bald Sinead O'Connor, sinfully censorious Rev. Don Wildmon, and other friends of the enemies of the powers that be?

The elevator opened into a large reception area. I asked a horse-eyed secretary if Mr. Whitlock were available. She looked at my stumpy body, read my unclean T-shirt, "GOD SAVE THE QUEEN, SHE AIN'T A HUMAN BEING," and asked if I had an appointment. I don't make mistakes twice. Damn right I did. I assumed a Benny Hill-like accent and introduced myself as Wilbur Whitlock, a distant cousin in town for the infamous San Gennaro festival.

She told me to have a seat and got on the horn. Since the seating area was out of sight and adjacent to a large, open space, filled with secretaries, computers, and stenography machines, I disappeared into this clerical quagmire, and watched, and waited. Overworked, the horse-eyed receptionist was completely unaware that I had disappeared.

In a moment, a tornado of people swirled into the reception area. Aides, subordinates, and secretaries flanked the dashing, late, late middle-aged rajah, Whitlock. Every moment of his existence had to be transformed into minutes, records, and notes, enough to assemble a pyramid of documentation. Through the nebulous mass of sidekicks, I caught glimpses of Whitlock. He resembled pieces of Warren Beatty, Mick Jagger, and Jack Nicholson—all fused together under a sunlamp.

Apparently, he had made this trip to the reception area to meet his distant cousin in person. I assumed this after he conducted an extensive interview with the horse-eyed receptionist, presumably concerning my whereabouts. He looked around and waited a moment. I watched her shrug ignorantly. About fifty thousand dollars later—time was money—he slipped back into his carpeted snakehole. An elevator suddenly whipped open its mirrored doors; I raced in past the receptionist.

"Sir!" Horse-eyes neighed after me. The elevator closed, dropped, and let me loose. Around pillar and post I lingered. Five o'clock released them: those-who-had-traded-their-shots-at-immortality-for-a-suit. I scoured through them. Identical suits in slightly different shades of gray gushed out of the elevators in life-raft-sized crews streaming homeward.

The clock ticked on. No sign of him; the living Reactor who transformed lives into money. I bided my time with wonder. Should I go right to violence: a knee-capping, Red Brigade-style abduction, a bit of bondage, and assassination a la Bader-Meinhof? Maybe something less dramatic, a Beirut kidnapping in which I'd just sedate him for the remainder of his natural life with tranquilizers. Or dared I try to reason with the beast?

Before I could decide, he beamed down. I instantly recognized him on an upper balcony. A Mussolini without a downward-draping flag. He paused regally as he surveyed his small army returning to its bivouac for the night. Each worker was a brush stroke on the master's canvas. Exiting the building, he carried the thinnest briefcase I had ever seen. He moved in quick lines, like a back-row chess piece. I followed at a distance. He tried to hail a cab, but there were none. Why no car was waiting for him, I couldn't fathom. He finally gave up and just walked. As we pressed through TriBeCa and up through a section of Chinatown, the streets became mysteriously empty. An opportunity was slowly unveiling itself. Soon, the two of us had the streets to ourselves. It was a study in contrast: he had billions, I had only bills.

The hour of vengeance was upon him. I increased my pace, closing in for the kill. Street sounds faded with the daylight. As we walked on those antique cobblestones of SoHo, only the hollow echo of our footsteps could be heard. Gradually, he sensed that he was being followed. He took casual detours and caught glimpses of me, a distorted figure in storefront windows. I watched him trying to remain calm; panicking might hasten his abduction. Soon, he started picking up his pace.

Like a master hunter, I could feel his heart slamming around in his chest, trying to get out. Like the gnu stalked by the lioness, he knew that wherever I finally intersected with him would be his death. Anxiety was having a field day: *STAB OUT MY EYES, CRUNCH THE BONES IN MY LIMBS, RIP OUT MY TONGUE, BUT END THE TORTURE!* Stripped of office rank and the brigades of subordinates, divested of communicative services and computer hookups, estranged, unplugged, deprived, and cut off from all his engines, generators, resources, strategies, and foot soldiers, the emperor wasn't merely naked, he was nude.

Faster he walked. His body lurched and jerked. He tried to run but the leash of reason held tight. Just walk faster, faster! It was like watching a silent film. I slapped my shoes hard on the pavement, giving the impression I was finally swooping down on the trembling bunny. Finally, he threw down the paper-thin briefcase and broke into a run. But suddenly, the pavement rose and tripped him into a muddy puddle.

He floundered a moment, but his large arms hoisted him from the ground. It was then that I realized that he was truly big, no, large, no, towering. When he slipped back into the puddle, falling sideways, he resembled a collapsed crane. Twice my size, pillowed in muscles: If he had ever turned to face his rock-slinging David, he'd have seen that there was nothing to fear but fear itself. I walked away discreetly yet triumphantly.

"Hey," I heard a thunderous bellow. Springing to his feet, he had finally mustered the courage to face the enemy. Yikes!

I raced, he chased. I dashed to West Broadway and skedaddled into some artsy-fartsy gallery. I ducked behind a postmodern, primitive expressionist piece. He soon loomed from behind a neoclassical sculpture. I raced back outside, into the Rizzoli Bookstore, and up the long flight of steps, squealing, "Help! Help!"

At the top step, I grabbed a huge, hundred dollar art book and held it above my head like a mighty boulder. He stood at the base of the steps below.

"He chased me," Whitlock explained to the security guard who was holding him at the base of the stairs. "He tried to steal my wallet or something."

"That's crazy," I said, still holding the book menacingly.

"Just don't hurt the book," the security guard appealed. Whitlock turned and stormed out. After a moment, I put the art book down and left. I had scored one for the little people. Thankless and un-laureled, I returned home. It had been a long day.

CHAPTER TWO
ONLY FART
WHEN EXITING

T he next afternoon, I went to Professor Flesh and pleaded for some minuscule-interest, ceaselessly long-term payment arrangement for my last semester registration fees. He said he was the wrong person to appeal to; however, my presence was required in the place where such decisions and revisions were made—Low Library.

"Why? Who knows about me?" I asked.

"I just got a phone call requesting the presence of the Whitlock Fellowship recipient, and you were the last dinosaur of that species."

"Do you think it might be an eleventh-hour reprieve?"

"I'll cross my fingers." He illustrated the point and told me the room in which I was to report.

Eagerly, I went back to Low, past the angst-filled security guard, who confirmed my appointment. I located the room. A pretty secretary kept vigil out front. I noticed a Hadassah calendar on the wall behind her, a fellow tribesman.

"Aeiou is the name," I said suavely, "reinstatement of the Whitlock Award is the game."

"You're the creep I spoke to yesterday," she started in.

"I spoke to you? What's your name?"

She held up a name plaque—Veronica. Young, chipper,

smartly dressed, she looked like a personals ad from the *Christian Herald Trombone.*

"I kind of lost myself yesterday. That was my telephone persona," I said amorously. "I hope you didn't take anything I said to heart."

"Actually, I was quite amused."

"How's that?"

"Well, I never heard anyone use insults so creatively. I was particularly touched by your attempt to try and find out my nationality."

I explained that I was a bit of a historian and that I had the dirt on every nationality. "No people are free from some kind of guilt."

"I'm a history major here, too." She explained that she was on foreign exchange from Israel.

"No kidding," I said, nodding my head Michael-J.-Foxishly, "maybe we can get together. Interpret the Talmud."

"I'd like that," she replied, and then notified the Dean that I was there. She listened for instructions, then hung up and told me to enter.

I opened the door. Two men were standing very quietly before large windows in a darkly-lit room filled with polished-walnut furniture. Sunlight was pouring in behind them.

"Hi, guys," I said.

"That's him," a deep bellow of masculinity made identification. My eyes and ears instantly adjusted. I realized that before me was Whitlock the Goliath, whom I had brought down just yesterday. If this meeting had taken place in the subway or on the street, I'm sure they would've beaten the shit out of me. But in such a nice room, with pipe smoke and heavy brocade drapes, they'd no doubt elect to go through legal channels.

"First of all," I began my defense, "I didn't do anything."

"I never said you did," Whitlock replied calmly.

"You fell down of your own volition. Admit it! You panicked on your own! Admit it!"

"So I did."

"When you chased me into Rizzoli's, you scared me; don't deny it 'cause you did."

"I probably did," he conceded.

"No judge or jury would ever believe a tiny person like me would try to accost a tall, Olympian like you."

"Absolutely."

"You're a witness! You're a witness!" I exclaimed to the Dean.

"Have a good day, Mr. Aeiou," replied the Dean.

"May I ask who the hell you are?" I said to the Dean.

"A dean; now leave my office," he said very calmly.

I walked back to Professor Flesh's office to try and work something out tuition-wise. But when I entered Flesh's office, he said he'd just received a phone call ordering him to bar me from the building. Furthermore, all my academic records with the university were seized, pulled, and probably shredded. That included my baccalaureate transcripts, so I couldn't even transfer to another school.

"That's illegal!" I hollered.

"I was only following orders," replied the history professor.

I dashed back to Low Library and past Veronica into the Office of the Dean of Covert Operations. They were both still there, bathed in shadows, hushed tones, phlegmatic laughter, and facelifts.

"Please, Mr. Whitlock." I threw myself to the ground. "I'm sorry for what I did, I beg you to have mercy."

"Notify campus security," the Dean said to Veronica, who entered behind me. She nodded with a smirk and left the room.

"Let me clarify something," he said. "I'm doing you a favor."

"What?"

"I could hurt you a lot more."

I kept begging, but the man kept ignoring me. He was talented at it. Arrogantly, he inspected a gilded portrait of some rich cocksucker. Soon the campus security, the large dumb animal in a uniform, grabbed me and forced both my hands behind my back. He pushed me out. As the security guard walked me past Veronica, she murmured, "Call me."

He took me to the phony-marble steps and let me calmly return to my decimated life. I walked down the steps and took a seat on a marble bench near the small, dry, penis-shaped fountain donated by alumna Margaret Dodge.

What the hell, I thought. Ever since I'd entered the graduate program I had pondered over a subject for a thesis. I was supposed to write one this semester and I had neither the subject nor the inclination; it was a good time to be thrown out of school. What was I going to do with a masters, except bullshit around academia? Maybe try for a teaching spot in some exclusive Alpine girls school, like Sly Stallone in his pre-*Rocky* days, and try to do as many of the religiously crippled virgins as possible? Be that as it may, this expulsion put some new possibilities into what otherwise might have been a life of joy and waste. As I passed through the gates donated by alumnus George Delacorte, I thought to myself, I can't let all this go. I mustn't. I took the subway downtown to Whitlock's office and waited outside of his glass-and-steel castle. An hour passed and then another, just like the first. A succession of limos came and went, until finally the door of one opened, and he got out.

"I beg you, Mr. Whitlock," I said, running up to him. His driver walked in interference between him and me.

"I only meant to appeal to you, but you kept walking away," I shouted around the stocky driver. But Whitlock walked toward the rhombus-shaped building and wouldn't even look at me.

"Please, Mr. Whitlock, you are obviously a very powerful man, but don't you agree that, in the words of that innovative financier Michael Milken, 'with power comes the veneer of responsibility'"—Milken, who used three-card monte as a model for the investment banking industry, never said any such thing, but I figured that Whitlock might respect one of his own—"For a miscalculation on my part, you're sentencing my whole life to incompletion! I beg you...I had no preconceived plan, and whatever embarrassment or damage I might have caused you was, ironically, only self-inflicted by your humongous ego."

But Whitlock entered his palace without acknowledging my words.

Upon my entering the building, security blocked my entrance. I took position across the street and waited out of view, watching covertly. Another hour came and went before Whitlock exited the building. I raced over. This time, his driver grabbed me and cranked his arm back, about to punch.

"No!" said Whitlock.

"Mr. Whitlock, I am not going away. I will be here every day, every waking hour, until you rethink this!"

"I am warning you. Leave me alone."

"I can't. You hold my future. I will be here every day, I warn you. Mr. Whitlock, Andrew, if I may call you that, the worst thing you can do to a person is to empower him and then knock that power away."

"You think so?" he asked matter-of-factly, and for the first time, he seemed to really hear me.

"Yes sir, absolutely." He smiled, got into his car, and drove away.

A tall order of sleep was the prescription. But New York was an awful city for sleep. Added to which, sleep had a bad rap. People who slept were assumed to be lazy. But sleep was the seat of man's power. His prophesies, his fantasies, his visitations to death, his real confrontations, his magical strength—all arose from sleep. And it was in sleep that I saw them: farmers in black pajamas, Asiatics racing around on a battlefield, scurrying into a myriad of tunnels, submerged under rice paddies. Learning the lesson of Vietnam, these pajama farmers defeated our mega-tech GIs. I realized a nothing-to-lose, grassroots guerilla operation was the only way to combat this.

It was morning of the next day, a good time to prepare for my Tet Offensive. I collected some of my late, unknown uncle's camping gear from around the house: a pup tent, a sleeping bag, a transistor radio, and a book on how to hold together under interrogation.

Manhattan on a map hangs like an old sock into the Narrows. I hopped on a bus to the big toe. Stopping by a Korean grocer, I acquired food staples, a cup of coffee, a black magic marker, and some cardboard boxes. Then I set up base camp on the sidewalk across from the rhombus building— Whitlock Incorporated.

I broke open the boxes and created instant placards (I love that word—placards). Using the magic markers, I scribbled my message to the world:

ANDREW WHITLOCK, WHO WORKS ACROSS THE STREET, USED HIS POWERFUL POST TO RUIN MY LIFE, BECAUSE HE THOUGHT I WAS GOING TO MUG HIM. ASK ME ABOUT IT. DONATIONS ENCOURAGED!

I put down a donation cup and set up the cardboard signs so any passerby could see them. For the first couple of minutes, I considered other fronts to fight on: The media eats up shit like this. If I could write a press release and fax it around, I was sure they'd send out one of those vans with the satellite dish on the roof. Then there were the talk show circuits; I could easily get on *Jerry Springer*. If I handled it right, I could even work my way down to *Geraldo*.

After fifteen minutes, I considered the possibility of writing a book proposal. This could be for me what the NEA grant-yanking had been for Karen Finley and the "defunded four." I pitched out a working title: *Let Me Learn in Peace! The Joe Aeiou Story.*

After twenty minutes, I started getting cold, and I realized that no one had stopped to even glance at my signs. My signs needed spicing up, so I scribbled, "Whitlock killed JFK!"

I unrolled the pup tent and decided to let time do its work. I cocooned myself within, plugging my transistor radio into my head, trying to find WBAI to hear the latest development of the war against the rich. Soon, though, I wound my way to the magical kingdom of sleep until the baton of one of New York's Finest woke me up by patting along the ribs of the tent, ergo my ribs (New York's Finest what?).

I felt an increasing frustration as I broke camp. When I was folded and packed, I bee-lined to the nearest payphone. I didn't know Whitlock's number offhand, and probably wouldn't be able to get him to come to the phone, so I decided to call that Dean and tell him that I wouldn't attend his flea-ass, matchbook school if he sucked a token out of my turn-stile. But as soon as I heard the juicy voice of his secretary, Veronica, my heart started farting, and my eyes palpitated.

"Is that you, AEIOU?" She pronounced my name lovingly.

"Hi, I was just wondering..."

"You little sex pod."

"I thought maybe..."

"Where do you want to meet?"

"Well, I figured..."

"Tower Books on Lafayette Street and Fourth at 6:00. Till then, you little love ghoul." Click. She must have been in season. I wasted no time in getting up there. I hung out for six hours, browsing through their anything-goes porn/zine section.

"Joseph!" she surprised me suddenly, sending that month's issue of *Tattooed Cycle Sluts* whizzing through the air. I grabbed an over-testosteroned copy of *World Wrestling Federation Magazine.*

"I wasn't looking at nothing!"

"I don't care," she said. But they really do: They want boys sanitized, slim, silent, and smiling.

We ended up going to some pretentious over-priced bistro where we sipped teeny demitasses of "micrappacini." She talked a storm, and although I understood every word she said, I couldn't piece them into sentences. I nodded a lot, smiled a lot, and kept looking for excuses to accidentally touch her body parts. When we finished our drinks, we walked around the skeletal remains of the once-exciting Village. By nightfall, we wound up kissing in Washington Square Park. I tried to feel her boobs, but...

"I have to know you better first," said she.

"Why? Even if I turn out to be a mass murderer, it'll still be me."

She said she would let me feel the outlying parts of one breast, but no nipple. I asked her if I could trade it to feel her Golan Heights, just a couple upper lockets. I had just read *The Art of the Deal*, and this is how The Don made it.

"I'll let you feel my armpits," she cleverly countered.

"Both pits?" I raised the ante.

"I suppose," she said, after a limited reluctance.

"Can I trade one of those pits for a Gaza Strip?"

"This is crazy!" Suddenly angry, she dashed out of the park via the walkway where five people had been killed by that runaway car. As I raced up University Place to catch up to her...

"Aeiou," I suddenly heard someone slide down the circular vowel congregation of my last name. Whitlock was waving at me from a slowly cruising limo.

"Come with me," he summoned.

"I'm on a date, sir," I replied to the *deus ex limo*.

"We have an understanding," Whitlock said. I wasn't certain if he was talking to me or Veronica, but she insisted that she had to go home now anyway and wanted to walk there alone.

"But I'm obliged to walk you home," I explained to her.

"This could be your reinstatement," she whispered, pushing me toward his tacky-ass batmobile.

He threw open the door. I assumed a seat next to him and unsuccessfully tried to evict a fart. Without a word, he took out a pocket cassette and replayed the conversation we had had in the Dean's office earlier that day, right down to my "ooofff" sound when the security guard yanked my arms behind my back. The limo made a right on Waverly Place and drove down Broadway as he spoke.

"What you don't understand, Aeiou, is that I am both judge and jury."

"Yes, sir."

"Your little appeal was quite persuasive. It touched me."

"Thank you." The false Milken quote must've worked.

"I'm referring to your encampment. I saw you outside my office today. I had the cop scare you off."

"Oh?"

"If you had held your ground, I would've respected you more."

"But..."

"But I give you credit. You scared me more than I've ever been scared before, and that touched me. It says a lot for you."

"Sure."

"See, usually I have at least one bodyguard with me, and that was the one day that I decided to try and go for a walk. So you can understand when I heard you behind me, I assumed it was someone who had deep access to my schedule, someone with true econ-political motives."

"I didn't..."

"Real revenge takes time, planning. You have to study someone to really hurt them."

"Oh, I know."

"I was certain I was dead when I realized you were following me. I mean I was never more afraid in all my life. And for that I want to thank you." He took my hand and shook it.

"You're welcome."

"You blasted away all the calcification that comes with cash. I actually forgot terror, fear. Began to think of myself as a god. You made me mortal again. Returned death to me. So anyway, I've reconsidered several rulings." I prayed as he spoke.

"I pieced together that you learned of my identity and resented my rescinding the family grant." He took out a small notebook as he spoke: "Fifteen hundred hours (3:00 p.m.): You called my secretary pretending to be a bike messenger."

Again he flipped through his Day Timer and checked the military-timed schedule of that misbegotten day.

"Around sixteen hundred (4:00 p.m.), you arrived claiming you were a cousin from England." 1588 was the destruction of the Spanish Armada.

"You spotted me when I came out to the waiting area. Yes or no?" I didn't remember anything but decided to plead guilty and rely on his mercy.

"Yes, sir."

"Then you followed me when I left my office sometime between seventeen hundred (5:00 p.m.) and seventeen thirty (5:30 p.m.). Perhaps you didn't mean to scare me. It is frankly a sensation that I hadn't experienced since the last great market correction. It's usually a role I put others in. This was like a jolt, quite traumatizing. You were very fortunate; I used to carry a Glöck. Is there anything further you want to tell me in your defense?"

"Just that I was desperate, and did something out of character, and am more than willing to pay any kind of penance."

"Anything else?" He wanted more.

"I'm very delicate, I have a weak heart."

"Yes."

"And…and you're very mighty and will live long, and I might have subconsciously resented that."

"Perhaps." He thought a moment before speaking. "Well, maybe I was a bit too harsh in condemning you. But I can't simply reinstate you. You did do an injustice to me and you do deserve punishment." He paused again and finally issued, "No, I can't let you back into my college."

"But what will I do, sir?"

"You have a part-time job at the Strand Bookstore, don't you?"

"Yes, but it's only for added indulgences. It's not enough to live on. My existence was founded on your stipend."

"Is that your girlfriend?" Whitlock pointed into the distance, referring to Veronica.

"No, I just bumped into her." I didn't want to expose Veronica to anyone other than myself.

"She certainly knows how to manipulate information."

"Pardon?"

"Relatives?"

"No, I'm adopted."

"Well," he paused and looked silently, directly into my eyes for so long I thought he was going to kiss me. "Who said that the cruelest punishment is actually the finest rehabilitation?" Not the same person who said that to err is human and to forgive is divine, I thought.

"It's time you worked in the real world. Ever read Thoreau? Self-reliance—that's the key."

It was funny he should use that phrase; Mr. Ngm via Mrs. Ngm had been throwing that phrase in my face for a long time. "What's it the key to?"

"We have to consider your aptitudes and altitudes."

Although I had never given him my number, he called me at home later that night.

"What are you doing tomorrow?" he said without introduction.

"The usual. Who is this please?"

"I want you to call in sick, and come by my little shop tomorrow. Don't come later than, oh, say nine hundred hours. I want to hire your services, my boy." And he hung up without saying goodbye.

The next day, I somehow succeeded in waking before noon and grabbed a train downtown. It was back to the rhombus building.

I sped up to the horse-eyed secretary and gave my name. By the jaundiced expression, it was safe to assume that she recognized me. Before letting me enter Whitlock's office, she pointed me to an empty conference room. "In the closet of that conference room are three suits. Mr. Whitlock wants you to put on the one that fits best. Then report to him. And you better hurry up, he's going to be taking off in twenty-five minutes."

Although I tried on all three garments, they didn't vary much in tightness-of-torso or floppiness-of-extremities. I put on the one that best complimented my butt, but had to leave my waist unbuttoned and roll up the sleeves and cuffs.

The horse-eyed secretary pulled out a Polaroid camera and inexplicably took a flash photo of me. Then she shoved me toward his office door. "Quickly, he's waiting for you."

I entered a room with a dozen men and women seated at a conference table. A magic marker board was vibrating with multi-colored arrows and notes. Prospectuses and presentations were spiral-bound before everyone.

Whitlock was sitting at the helm of the table, facing away from all, staring out on that fabulous view of the East River bracketed by the Brooklyn and Manhattan Bridges. The FDR vanished at his feet. I noticed a refreshment table, complete with coffee, a plate of bagels, bialys, lox, cream cheese, donuts, and so forth. I quickly went over, poured myself a coffee, and started stuffing donuts and other delectables into my pockets.

"Can we help you?" one of the execs asked me in a 'What-the-fuck?' tone.

"Is that you, Joey?" Whitlock asked before I could answer. He was still staring in the direction where great destroyers were once assembled, the Brooklyn Navy Yard, away from all.

"Yes sir," I sputtered through a mouthful of donut.

"Everyone, this is Joey," he introduced, "the efficiency man I warned you all about."

"Efficiency man?" I repeated.

"What department do you plan to look at first?" one of them inquired nervously.

"Oh, I don't know," I said, chewing down some herring in cream sauce.

"Joey's not doing a systematic; he does sporadics. Here and there. He'll pop in, peruse, and vanish like sand, only reporting to me," Whitlock said. Then, turning around dramatically, he added, "Joey might look like an odd combination of grunge and suit, but that's because he's an unincrementalized genius."

"Well..." I sputtered modestly as stuff fell out of my mouth.

"Right now, though, me and Jojo have a plane to catch," Whitlock said, and bouncing up, he trotted out the door. I moved quickly on his heels.

Out the corridor to an awaiting elevator, the horse-eyed wonder accompanied us. In the elevator, without even asking me, she clipped a laminated ID to my suit pocket. On the ID was the face photo she had taken of me with her Polaroid.

"Where are we going?"

"Several stops," he said. With that he took a tiny cellular phone out of his pocket and talked in whispers as we moved through that hi-tech cavern of a lobby, out the automated door, and into an awaiting limo. Still on the phone, we zoomed up the FDR to a heliport. Still on the phone, we hopped into an awaiting chopper. A little desk was set up. He was still absorbed in his hushed conversation. On the desk top: a *Wall Street Journal*, *New York Times*, a fax machine, a box of Havana cigars. In the cup that held sundry writing instruments, I spotted a platinum-topped, midnight blue, Montblanc pen that had to be worth at least twenty-five bucks. Up until then, I had devoted the time to wolfing down the food that I had stuffed in my pockets. But as the helicopter approached landing at JFK Airport, I polished off my snack and made my way to his end of that tight cabin, near the little efficiency desk.

"So what say you, Jojo?"

"Really something," I said, awestruck. He gave me a powerful slap on the back and turned to his left just long enough for me to reach into that leather-wrapped pencil cup and snatch the Montblanc. Landing, we got out with the chopper blades still revolving and ran across a tarmac into a large, awaiting corporate jet. When we got into the plane, he turned to me and said, "So are we having fun yet?"

"Sure," I replied. I got in my seat, over the wing, and tried on the headphones. Yes, I wanted breakfast. Yes, I wanted the steak lunch with the artificial grill marks. Yes, I wanted to see the film, though I already knew it was a dud, and I had probably seen it.

The plane soon took off. I looked down at that overpacked island, bordered between silver slivers of polluted rivers, a frail vein just waiting to burst like a cerebral hemorrhage, havoc in miniature. I had probably got out just in time. Several execs stood up at the tail of the plane and made presentations to Whitlock about various holdings and plans. He asked several questions; the secretary did several calculations. Once or twice, he got back on the cellular and confirmed some facts. Over the wing of the plane was a small bar, where I loaded up on a variety of courtesy drinks.

"Do you want to ask them anything about this deal?" Whitlock turned from the band of execs and asked me as I was pouring a small bottle of rum into my coke.

"I'm sorry, I really wasn't listening. I better sit this one out."

"These guys are proposing a two hundred million dollar investment in a string of manufacturing plants in Eastern Europe. We would be with a consortium of other American businesses."

"I see."

"Any questions for them, Jojo?"

"Well, if you buy all the cheap real estate in the area of the plants, you can open up diners and gas stations and stuff."

"Good point," Whitlock said without a hint of sarcasm. That was the last time he asked me if I had any questions. I was looking forward to all those plane frills. But soon after we were in the air, I drifted into a deep and productive sleep. When I awoke, I feared I'd missed the fun and quickly pushed the button for the stewardess. I was taken aback by her response time.

"Can I get my breakfast, lunch, and the film?"

"I'm sorry, but the pilot just turned on the no-smoking sign."

"I don't smoke."

"We're going to be in an angle of descent in a few minutes."

"Okay, just bring me a drink and some honeyed nuts."

"Sorry, sir, we're in descent." To avoid the issue, she then vanished down the aisle. With a bump and screech, we were in Washington.

Outside the terminal, a limo was waiting, identical to the one we'd left in New York. We drove past the Beltway, past the Vietnam Wall and a variety of other monuments. We finally arrived at an old office building and strode into another large office, to another meeting—a swirl of people who looked like those we'd just left in New York.

A series of presentations by counselors and consultants came and went, and soon, when my vanity—which compelled me to believe that I was all-knowing and all-powerful—finally faded, I wondered what the hell I was doing there. I ended up reading glossy, smelly women's magazines filled with jackass articles about How to Land a Husband next to declarations on the New Breed of Feminism. Around sixteen hundred hours (4:00 p.m.), Whitlock raced out of his final office and called to me, "Let's go."

"Where?"

"We're returning to Gotham." Limo to plane to New York to chopper to the city proper. During the entire journey, he divided his conversation between cellular phones, lackeys, and me, in that quantitative order. He let me loose at Times Square.

"Can I go back to school now?" I boldly asked him.

"Not quite, but here." He handed me a five dollar bill and his business card, and said, "Come to my home tomorrow. We'll have din-din."

"Can I at least get my transcripts and papers?"

"What are you talking about?"

I explained that the school was holding my transcripts and other vital papers. I was unable to transfer to another graduate school, even if I could manage to finagle the money.

"Okay, just come on time tomorrow," he replied. Then, turning to Horse-eyes, he said, "Secure the boy's papers. In the event I'm late, my man Wylie will look after you until I get in."

"Great." I got out, looked at the tourists, and went home.

(I could wax rhapsodic about the shades of sunlight creeping across symbolic objects of the figurative. I could produce metaphors and similes for the minute-stirring hours and the dissipation of the human spirit through sterile or rococo exercises in postmodernist prose style, but suffice it to say—) Time passed.

* * *

The next day, I walked across town to his house. I was fairly tired and dizzy. As I approached, a beggar from a nearby street corner followed me like a hungry dog, telling me pathetic details of his fictitious life.

"Hold it, now," I said, trying to locate the address. I should have given him the courtesy of a quick refusal, but he seemed to feel good telling about his ills, so I let him follow and talk. The address on Whitlock's business card brought me to an upper East Side town house with a beautiful row of steps out front. The beggar followed me up to the top step. I rang the bell and waited.

"Hey," my homeless companion said, "I have a life, too. You mind if I get on with it?" I gave the guy a dollar-fifty.

"Fuck you!" he yelled, just as some long white guy wearing a tarboosh opened the front door.

"Oh dear!"

"Fuck you!" I said to the homeless guy.

"Could you both please take your melee elsewhere," the long, white tarboosh-wearer replied, slamming the door shut.

"No, wait," I banged on the door. When he reopened it, the tarboosh was gone. I introduced myself to the doorman, shaking his hand, man-style.

"Who was that?"

"A crazy, I don't know. He followed me here," I replied. Delicately hinting that I wanted to be fed, I added, "Boy, am I hungry!"

"Oh, yes. I'm Wylie. Andrew informed me you'd be here around now. Come on upstairs, you chowhound, and let's get you chowed down."

It was apparent that not all was well in this man's state of Denmark. Wylie led me through a glorious brownstone: cherry wood paneling, furniture pieces that had been stolen from different periods, a rolled-up carpet from the Orient. The moldings were sculptured with haloed cherubs and demons with tongues twisted out. Banisters were dragons' heads. The fretwork of the baseboards and detail of the artwork seemed to improve with every upward landing. When we finally reached the top flight, he led me into a beautiful dining room, and said, "Take a seat. Whitlock and the meal will be here shortly."

"Do we have to wait?" I asked.

"I suppose not. Master Whitlock has already eaten."

I sat at the right side of a long dining table with two place settings. All I could think as he brought out a serving bowl was, I've spent twenty-four hours waiting for the feast in that bowl.

"Pass your…"—I did. As he started filling my plate, tears came to my eyes. When he slid the plate over in front of me, I stared down into a bowl of macaroni and cheese. I looked up at him, and watched as he spooned clumps of noodles onto his own plate. Then, placing the bowl in the center of the table, he proceeded to fork the noodles into his mouth. I smiled and did likewise. They tasted gooey and powdery.

"Jeepers, am I one hungry hound dog," Wylie said, as he tunneled through his plate of crap. Then, to himself he replied, "'Course you are."

When I discreetly spat my mouthful of macaroni into a napkin, I realized the cheese was made from a powder that wasn't quite mixed. Pushing my fork through the bowl, I spotted unmelted chunks of margarine and unblended clots of cheese powder.

"Say, what exactly is this?" I asked as politely as possible.

"Macaroni and cheese—eleven cents a serving! Isn't it wonderful?"

As I resentfully chewed it down, I couldn't help remembering that Whitlock—according to *Fortune*—was worth about $3,500,000 per year. Which means he must've made roughly $10,000 per day, seven days a week. Was spending $20 for a real dinner so exorbitant?

Maybe it wasn't Whitlock's fault. This Wylie character, Whitlock's manservant, was an obvious flake. He had incredibly white hair that looked like the belly feathers of a goose. His face was punctuated by spaces: gaping eye sockets, large red ears that resembled toilet plungers, a big cantaloupe-sized mouth with a stupid inbred grin. He bantered a strange preemptive conversation at me as I tried to eat.

"So how was your trip, young man?" He.

"Not…" Me.

"It was awful of course, you boob…" He.

"No, I didn…" Me.

"Don't ask me such dumb questions you say…" He.

"No, it's oka…" Me.

"Tell me what you can do for me, Wylie, and stop being such an old nuisance!" He.

"You weren't being…" He might have been insane but he wasn't dangerous, so I just listened to him talking to himself with a fictitious character representing an irate me.

"Why in heaven's name don't you go to the Walter Raleigh and play the Charles and Diana? Who's the Walter Raleigh, you say? Aren't Charles and Diana royal monarchs, you nincompoop? Indeed they are, my boy. Indeed they are. But, you see, I give inanimate things animated names. Inanimate names, you say? Yes I bloody do in fact…." He continued rambling as I snuck into the kitchen. It was new and clean, and held the promise of other foods. But when I opened the refrigerator, all I saw was a tub of margarine, a rotting onion bulb, and individually wrapped American cheese slices.

Suddenly, an electronic doorbell emitted the sound of birds chirping. It didn't have any effect on Wylie's external monologue which eternally continued, questioning and answering itself in strange, dialectical senility. Then Whitlock appeared in the doorway.

"Ahh, Mister Whitlock," Wylie muttered, "She's waiting for you downstairs."

"I'm a he, and I'm here," I corrected.

"Not you," Wylie replied.

"How are you?" I asked Whitlock, as I moved from the barren fridge to a sofa in the living room.

"Ahhh, *cestui que vie*." He sighed, flopped down next to me, and pressed my hand.

"Mr. Whitlock, I don't know what that Dean said about me, but…" I began nervously.

"Res ipsa loquitur."

"I just want to say that none of this was my idea."

"Molliter manus imposuit."

"I didn't do nothing wrong."

"Mallum prohibitum?"

"At least nothing I knew about."

"Ignorantia legis non excusat."

"I mean, I didn't mean to do what I did to you and, well, when I think about it, it makes me want to…" I caught myself.

"Exturpia causa non oritur actio."

"Yeah, well, it still makes me feel angry."

"Facinus quos inquinat aequat."

"Master Whitlock," Wylie spoke up, "the boy was in the middle of his noodle."

"This should take no more than a moment."

"What?"

"Your future." He murmured this as he vanished out the door. I pursued. He kept vanishing behind landings and doorways just as I got to them. All the while, he was talking confidentially about something I couldn't follow. Finally, at the ground floor, I entered a room to find him standing in a closet holding clothes, assessing them like a tailor.

"So, Wylie was making you dinner, was he?"

"Macaroni and cheese—eleven cents a serving."

"Apologies. If you wish to excuse yourself, the vomitorium is down the corridor to your left."

"It stayed down."

"Put this on, if you would. Bring your clothes and come with me."

"Where are we going?"

"Ours is not to question why…"

As he marched out of the room, he called back, "I'll be waiting outside." A pressed-yet-loose suit, a brand-new white shirt complete with pins in the collars, and a formal blue tie sat on an old Arts and Crafts armchair. Whitlock started walking again westward, back into the hall of the building with endless rooms. We marched through corridors and stairways. Finally, outside a large, old door, he stopped and waited for me.

"Here," he handed me a roll of breath mints. I slipped one into my mouth and took four for later.

"If you don't mind," he said, "I want you to agree with everything I say."

"God gave me a mind," I cowered courageously.

"No, no," he responded. "I just mean when we go into this room. We're visiting Mama and her society."

"Oh, I thought you meant in general, like about gun control and national health care. Sure, I'll go along."

He opened the door and we skipped in. An attendant was on duty. Inside were four ancient and sexless humanoids who all looked equally close to death laying side by side, yo-yo-ing between consciousness and all points north. Whitlock steered me toward the ghostly skeletal form by the window.

"How are we today, Mama? You look to be in top form…" Eight tubes were anchored to various parts of her drifting body, making her look like a sun-dried octopus.

"I dieeeee…" she muttered, or something like that. As far as I could figure, she was very, very tired, or paralyzed.

"Nonsense, you'll be dancing on my grave."

"Ahhhhh…" She should have taken better care of herself.

"Mama, do you know who I am?"

"Yahhh…"

"Mama, allow me to introduce my heir and protégé, Joseph Aeiou. Come here, Joey, and shake Mama's hand. He reached under a sheet and handed me a hand. It was weightless, cold, hard, and dark, like a wooden walking stick. I wondered for a moment if it was connected to anything.

"Pleased to make your acquaintance," I said cheerfully. What kept her alive? What kept all these people alive?

"Ahhhhhh…"

"Twenty-three. And how old are you?" I asked. She hadn't asked my age, but I had to know hers. She had an extraordinary translucence. I wanted to know how long one had to live in order to get that.

"Mama is 103 years old."

"Wow! You know, that weatherman on NBC's *Today Show* will announce your birthday on the air if you tell him."

"Mama was suspended in the air by Queen Victoria."

"No fooling!"

She smiled faintly.

"The Queen, in the last year of her life, held mama, who, at the time, was in the first year of hers."

"No kidding."

The silver lady nodded yes. Suddenly, some elderly guy in a clerical collar was standing at the door.

"Ah, I see you have another visitor. We shan't keep you. Ta-ta, Mother." And we were out of there. He led me back through the corridors to the room with the closet.

"Change back into your clothes, and let's figure out a racket for you."

"I don't want to sound uppity," I explained, "but I always wanted to do a little more with my life. And I'm not really a scholar."

"I see what you're saying."

After I changed back into my clothes, Whitlock went behind a small bar where a tiny refrigerator was hiding. Reaching inside, he took a tunafish sandwich wrapped in cellophane and offered it to me. "I have a gift for finding people's vocations. If you have a calling, I'll see it in your eyes."

"Well, I can certainly use the help." The tunafish tasted like chicken salad.

"All right, kiddo, tell me if I'm wrong. You're looking for a profession that is wide open. Good money. Shot at the top. And a shot at your name being carved into stone. Yes or no?"

"That's it."

"Okay, kiddo, I've got the answer right here, but I got to tell you something. Nothing comes without its price, without its trade-off." It was chicken salad.

"What do you want?" I asked him.

"Not a thing. The trade-off will be the job I'm going to tell you that fits that area."

"If you're going to tell me a high-labor, risky job…"

"This job allows you to sit on your caboose most of the time: unlimited booze, TV, housekeeper, free wardrobe. And although you need to attend another, different kind of graduate program, you can virtually start this job tomorrow."

"I'm interested."

"The priesthood."

"You're joking, right?" When I had finished the sandwich, Whitlock took two cans of soda from the fridge, one for him and one for me.

"A little, but not in the main, no. Let me weigh some of the pros and cons for you. First of all, there's an employee shortage. Second, you can work anywhere in the world. Third, you have high respect within the community. With a little politicking you can rise up the ranks to Bishop, Cardinal, maybe even to the top-dog seat. They're now hiring non-natives. Also, you cheat taxes and maybe death."

"I don't think so."

"Just give it some thought."

"I don't believe in God," I nullified.

"*De Minimus*. I don't believe in the law. This isn't a theological discussion—it's employment counseling."

"Look, I appreciate the suggestion, don't misunderstand me. I'd just feel like I was pulling a big con job." I finished my soda, and he started walking me somewhere. Again, I followed faithfully.

"I'm a lawyer. People come to me asking for confidence in matters that no one can give them confidence in. But I let them get things off their chest. I give them the best counsel I can. If I had to be honest, it would be a very, very bleak world indeed. You shouldn't be insincere, but find a pragmatic angle to help others." We were now at the front door, and his man Wylie was waiting there with my coat.

"Take care, my boy," he said.

"What now?" I asked, feeling like an umbrella asking where its owner was taking him.

"Even though you don't know this, you are presently going through a complete thought scrub."

"What's a thought scrub?"

"I have a tank of people working on your problem. And when the problem is worked out, you'll be notified. Go home now. Digest your macaroni and cheese. Sleep."

"What about my vital papers?"

"Oh, glad you mentioned them." He vanished a moment and returned with a large, plain, brown paper bag. Inside were my transcripts and a variety of vital statistics about me.

I went home, to sleep. Sleep inverts time. Sleep a few seconds, they seem like hours. Sleep hours and they seem like seconds. I awakened what seemed like moments later to a knock at my door. I wondered if I hadn't somehow caught a dose of muscular dystrophy or cerebral palsy. Some of me just wasn't responding to the messages from central command. My fingertips and toes were wiggling but the longer muscles wouldn't cooperate. I couldn't get the door, but apparently it was unlocked. A bike messenger entered and saw me lying on my bed wiggling and blinking.

"You okay, man?"

"I...don't know, don't know...sick...me sick..."

I remembered the last thing I ate was that cellophaned sandwich at Whitlock's place. "I ate chicken or tuna."

"It's probably your cavities, man."

"Huh?"

"They've discovered a bunch of problems stemming from metalloid cavities. Do you have metalloid or ceramic cavities?"

"Dunno."

"Let me look." The nut looked in my mouth.

"Metalloid! I don't want to be an alarmist, but you might consider getting them replaced with ceramic."

"Okay."

"You want to sign for this? I got other stuff to deliver."

"Okay."

He put a pen in my hand; I wiggled it against a clipboard. He put down a parcel and left.

I slept for an untold conspiracy of hours. By the afternoon, I had reached the shores of semi-consciousness. In an effort to arise, I fell to the floor. I stumbled to the bathroom, stepped on a cockroach, and peed in a series of short and confusing lines. I opened the parcel I had signed for in my dream state. It was a copy of a book, *My Saber Is Bent* by Jack Paar. There was a note inside: "It's solved! Call me—Whitlock."

Without any interest in speculating what it could be, I called him. His secretary informed me that he had been waiting for me to call all day and she put me right through.

"Is that you, Joey?"

"Yes, it's me, Joey."

"We've got it. Ready for this? Are you ready for it?" He was speaking too fast for a response: "How would you like a job that you can work whenever you like. It'll make you oodles of money. You'll enjoy it. You'll be in control and you don't have to say any mass or anything."

"Well, I..."

"A stand-up comedian."

"A stand-up comedian?!"

"I have a friend; he owns a very popular night club. He books comics. I can get him to give you a break."

"I don't know the first thing about comedy."

"You're a natural."

"I haven't the foggiest notion of..."

"Public speaking," he cut me off, "specifically the art of amusing an audience, is essential to a winning personality."

"I depress people..."

"Look, I'll get you a ten-minute spot on one of his amateur

nights. Read up on the topic. Nobody'll expect a thing from you."

"I really don't think so."

"I'll tell you what," he muttered. "I'll give you recommendations and tell you exactly how to get a job that pays three times the wage you're making now at the bookstore. You won't have to see me again, and there's a lot of down time."

"Down time? As what, a scuba diver?"

"It's a proofreading job."

"What's down time?" I asked.

"Time when you're not working, but getting paid for it."

"Why are you doing this?" I asked.

"Did you get the book?" He ignored my question.

"The Jack Paar book?"

"Yeah, he's my fave. Just learn some jokes and be yourself. You'll knock 'em dead, son. And remember, there are agents in the audience."

His secretary got on to fill me in on some background details. I was to meet Mr. Whitlock in seven days for an amateur night at what he referred to as a classy uptown nightclub called *YUK!*

CHAPTER THREE
HE WHO LAUGHS LAST
THINKS SLOWEST

I wrote a couple of jokes and tried practicing them in front of a mirror. I called Veronica and told her that Whitlock and I had bonded, and he was helping me with the underdeveloped parts of my life.

"Did he reinstate your grant?"

"No, but he is going to help me break into a new career."

"How?"

"I'm going to do a stand-up comedy routine at a club in upper Manhattan called *YUK!*"

"What?"

"It sounds kind of weird, but it can lead to good money and, more importantly, I'm trying to get into his good graces."

"Where and when will this occur?"

I told her when and gave her the address of the club and said that if she wanted to meet me there we could go on a date afterwards.

"Listen," she broke in, "you better be careful."

"Of what?"

"Well, I shouldn't be telling you this, but…" Her line went dead. When I called her back at work, the line was busy. I figured I'd see her at *YUK!*

At the appointed time, I dressed well, popped a couple of muscle-relaxants and anti-depressants, and went to *YUK!* It turned out to be a filthy, stuffy, overpriced dump with the kind of audience that goes to Karaoke bars. When I decided that this wasn't for me and turned to go, a very large-backed guy approached me.

"You look lost," he said.

"I always look that way. I was just leaving."

"What? Did we offend you?" he replied, threateningly.

I explained that I was a friend of Andrew Whitlock.

"The philanthropist, sure. We was expecting you." He put his shaggy arm around my bad back and walked me through the crowded audience, up a short, dark flight of steps. I thought he was taking me to Whitlock's table until suddenly a spotlight came on, and I realized I was on a stage. Picking up the mike, he said, "Folks, a loud round of applause for the comical investigations of Joseph Aeiou!" He then left me alone there. They started applauding for no reason at all.

I nervously recited a joke, "Why are Jews such rough lovers? `Cause they're not Gentile."

That joke was an insider for Veronica, but I didn't see her. Others, mainly from the bar, moved over by the stage. I went through my short list of set-piece jokes. Soon the manager with the shaggy arm had to knot on an apron and assist the waitress. The audience seemed to be a homogeneous group of some kind. Were they the Elks? Maybe the Rotary Club? I didn't recall any tour buses parked outside. After a punch line, I shielded my eyes from the spotlight and searched for Veronica. I couldn't see her. I then searched for some common thread that might suggest the audience was unified. Were they all wearing Viking-horn hats? Maybe they were Oriental. Nothing was apparent.

"I'm the only comic that impersonates a clitoris," I said, and stuck out my tongue tip just a bit at the right side of my wet, sealed lips. Then I tilted the left side of my face down, so that my mouth was vertical. A staunch silence roared, but then I heard a single girlish giggle. It was the sound of nervous embarrassment for someone else—Veronica's tender titter.

Unintentionally, her laugh seemed to permit an onslaught of laughs and foot stomping. Noticing a clock on the far wall, I realized with utter relief that my ten minutes were up.

"Thank you very much," I said. As the houselights went up, I found a standing ovation before me.

From nowhere, the manager was up on the stage alongside me, yelling into the mike, "What do you say we give our champ one more round!" All cheered.

"I'm outta material," I whispered to the manager, but he had dashed off, beyond hearing, back to servicing the tables. I was alone. The intermission had ended, and the spotlight had pinned me back onto the stage. Not knowing what else to do, I started feeling through my shirt pocket. I had purchased a magic card deck in the event that something like this might arise. I nervously undid the wrapper and realized that I had never bothered to learn the tricks. Spinning about-face, I started reading the instructions, 'To operate the magic card deck…'

Behind me, all the while, I could hear a steady seepage of laughter. After several minutes, the instructions were only getting more confusing, and even though the audience was still laughing, I was getting increasingly nervous. I finally tried slipping the instructions back into my pocket, but accidentally dropped them on the floor. There was no time to pick them up. I began yanking other things out, looking for something else to joke about. My wallet, matches, keys, loose change—all dropped to the floor. People kept laughing, but it was bad laughter. They were laughing at the wrong things.

"What's so funny about that?" I finally had to ask. All laughed again.

"Look," I finally admitted, "I'm not a comedian, I work in a bookstore."

"A bookstore!" someone responded. People were choking on laughter.

"Yeah, a fucking bookstore. What's wrong with that?" What's wrong with that? I thought to myself. It was where life had led me. I was adopted and, like most everyone else, I was mistreated by emotionless parents. Cycles of grade school, high school, and college had done their work at building me up and grinding me down. Now all my self-esteem could buy was a part-time job organizing the forty-eight cent outdoor books at the Strand.

I could sleep late in the mornings and attend school in the afternoons, and I'd work out theories in history: the trends and cycles, the machinations of conspiracies, the mathematics of economies, the depletion of the American spirit, the diffusion of the American dream…. "Sometimes, I'll admit, at bored moments, when I'm daydreaming and shouldn't be held strictly responsible for my thoughts, I find myself pretending I'm other people and…and…" Shrieks of laughter from the audience made me realize that I had unintentionally muttered aloud all these intimate thoughts. I froze. I could feel my eyes melting with tears.

"That's enough," said the manager, who had climbed up onto the stage and was tugging at my sleeve.

"They've no business! That's my life they're laughing at!"

"Ah, son, they just want a laugh," he replied. The laughs were now like waves nearing high tide. They receded only to hit back harder. I snatched a beer bottle and threw it into the laughs.

"Hey," the manager whispered, "I'm liable if you hurt someone. Now I want you off my stage!" Then, into the mike the asshole announced, "Our next performer…"

Before he could finish his sentence, I shoved the manager off the stage into the tables below. Then, taking hold of the microphone and its stand in both hands, I swung it around once like a hammer-thrower and released it. Still the laughs washed in. I started screaming obscenities into the crowd. They kept laughing. Finally, I dropped to the floor in a seated position and buried my face between my knees and put my hands over my ears, closed my eyes, and wondered, what did I do to deserve this? Nothing! I had done nothing, and therefore nothing wrong. I lowered myself off the platform until I got caught on something. In fact, something was holding me.

"What's the idea of knocking me off the stage?" the gorilla manager asked, lifting me up by the belt of my pants. "You want it, it's yours." The manager tumbled me back onto the stage. I scrambled around to the stairs, but the manager raced around blocking my escape.

"Help!" I yelled, shielding my eyes from the glare. "Someone notify the police! Veronica, help!"

The laughs had taken charge. I could no longer see or hear her. I might as well have been standing on some desolate bridge. I just let go, collapsing into the dark pool of audience before me. I hit my head on something and just lay there.

"It's only stage blood," I vaguely heard someone say. Hands suddenly reached out of the darkness, grabbing me, applauding, slapping me softly.

"Give him air," the manager said, inspecting the gash on my forehead. I counted to three, and then with a hop I pushed the manager aside, took to my feet, and rushed out the door.

"Shit!" some guy screamed, and then chased me. Several people in the audience also pursued.

I raced down Second Avenue. They were going to drag me back inside and throw me up again on that stage of fire. They wanted more laughs. I could feel a trail of wetness, blood trickling down my forehead.

"They're laughing at me! They're laughing at me!" I yelled, but no passerby helped. They only dodged me. I finally raced down onto a subway platform. Holding my wound, I boarded a train, the number six, packed with disparate, desperate New Yorkers, underscoring the sad fact that although people can break up, places cannot. New York was doomed to be locked together into one unharmonious circle of woe. When I finally got home, having lost enough blood to fill a pail, my phone was ringing. I answered it. Someone on the other end was laughing.

"Who is this? WHAT DO YOU WANT?!"

"Whitlock," he replied, "I saw your performance. I'm very proud of you. I had no idea you had that kind of talent."

"YOU WERE THERE?" I yelled. "Why didn't you help me? They tried to kill me."

"They loved you."

"They chased me!"

"They were running you like the bulls in Pamplona. I bet if you do it again next year, they'll make an annual event out of running you."

"I don't like being run. My head's bleeding."

"I'm giving you an extra five dollars for that. Who, by the way, is Veronica? At one point you yelled out, 'Help, Veronica.'"

"No one, just an expression I commonly employ in moments of despair."

"Oh, I've got good news."

"What?"

"The manager has told me that he'll book you again next week."

"No thanks. I'm never going to revisit that humiliation and pain."

"Actually, I have something else lined up as well."

"What?"

"An A.M."

"Ante Meridian?"

"Assistant Mortician in a funeral parlor in Brooklyn—Malio Funeral Home."

"No way."

"Think about it."

"It gets even more disgusting when I think about it."

"You might find a nice girl."

"Huh?"

"A nice girl." He paused, "You might meet a nice girl."

"What?"

"You might find yourself alone with her in a room together."

"I don't know what you're talking about."

"Yes, you do."

"I don't."

"Maybe, on second thought," he said, "a younger girl, or...boy, if that's what you're into."

"Where would I meet these people?"

"At the place of business."

"Huh?"

"You know, clients."

"What?"

"Meeting people. A little cold at first, a little strange, but you don't worry about convention, do you?"

"Huh?" I sensed that the patriarch had a couple of drinks in him.

"They can't really chat in their condition."

"Wait a second, what are we..."

"That's right."

"Huh?"

"That's right."

"Really?"

"Absolutely."

"Do you think..."

"Positively."

"Have you ever..."

"Who hasn't?"

"We're not talking about..."

"The exact same thing."

"Huh?"

"Huh, crap. You know exactly what I'm talking about."

"I don't."

"I think you do."

"You're disgusting," I said, which was followed by rigid

stalactites of laughter. I hung up the phone and went to wash my hands. His implications made me feel dirty. The phone rang. I lifted it and hung up, and then washed my face. Again, the phone rang. I hung up again, unplugged the phone, and cleaned it. Then I brushed my teeth, gargled. For some intuitive reason, I scrubbed my reagan. The next day, I plugged the phone into the wall outlet, and it rang immediately. I picked it up.

"Take it easy now, son."

I hung up and unplugged the phone again, then went to work at the Strand. After work that night, I came home, ate a banana, and read *The Prophet Unarmed* on the toilet (took a dump that resembled a deer's hoof). Soon it was 3:00 a.m. I plugged the phone into the wall outlet; it rang. I picked it up.

"Just listen to me a minute," Whitlock said. "I want to help you if you just let me." I hung up. It rang again. I picked it up and hung it up. It rang again. I picked it and hung up. It rang again. I picked and hung up, it rang again. I picked it and hung, rang again. I picked it hung, rung. I hung it rung…I rung, it hung…. Finally, I unplugged the phone, whanked off, and fell asleep with a gob of goo on my lower belly and a cockroach staring at me from a distant wall, befuddled.

About a week later, while sitting on some boxes in the Strand Bookstore, inspecting some "art-photography" books (thank god for the First Amendment!), I was called to the manager's office.

"Today, Joseph, this gentlemen has purchased your loyalty." He pointed to Whitlock, who was standing there dressed in military regalia.

"Hold it a second, I'm not a slave!" I hollered.

"No, but you are no longer employed with us," he explained. The manager left the room, and I was alone with the necro-bag.

"Now look what you did!"

"Do you know," he said nonchalantly, "that I could have you snuffed, no problem? But I'm not mad at you or anything."

"What do you want?"

"I'm sorry, I shouldn't have said that. The truth is I like you. But that incident left me a little twisted. I still have to work it out. You have to help me here."

"What are you, some kind of freak? This state has anti-stalker laws, you know."

"Relax. You're kind of my responsibility. I mean, you were living off my family award. You're an investment."

"Let's quit clowning around. You leave me alone, and I'll leave you alone."

"Come on, let's put it behind us and be best buddies." He extended his hand.

"Fuck you. Fuck the award. I got you real good. I'll always remember humiliating you, making you into a loopy sap. That'll be my contribution to humanity."

"You're right, this isn't over yet, is it?"

"It is for me."

"But don't you want your reward?"

"What reward?"

"The proofreading job. It's a piece of cake. Do it." He gave me the name and address of a law firm.

"Why are you doing this for me?" I asked.

"Two reasons. The first is you might learn something. You might begin to understand."

"Understand what?"

"Contracts, stipulations, riders, waivers."

"What about contracts?"

"Did you know everything can be reduced to contracts? Why, your life is a contract between two parent corporations."

"Don't include me in your scheme; I'm adopted."

"Then you were a contract unkept."

"What do you want from me?"

"I want to keep an eye on you. Maybe in a couple years, or whenever I feel you've served out your sentence, I'll have the

Dean lift your restriction. Who knows? Maybe I'll even rein-state your award."

"Fuck you, fuck the job, fuck the award. I got you real good. I'll quit with that."

I could see a glint of insanity in his right eye, like a cat with distemper. Then, he snickered and spoke, "You did that, m'boy. You did that. But are you a gambler?"

"What do you mean, a gambler?"

"I mean, would you like to continue this little contest, see who wins?"

"You might extract pain and suffering from me, but you'll never be able to do to me what I did to you."

"Come out to the car a minute. I want you to meet some-body, a friend of mine." I followed him out to his hearse. Standing in front of it, he said, "I want you to know that what I'm going to show you isn't personal. It's just something that kind of evens the score. If you want that proofreading posi-tion, it's still yours." I couldn't see in through the tinted glass of the car windows. He opened the door. Veronica was sitting there watching the compact TV and holding a frozen, lime-colored drink with a small parasol in it.

"Get out of the car, Ronnie. There's a friend here I'd like you to meet," he said.

"What, dear?"

"You have good taste, if you get my drift," Whitlock said to me. Veronica got out. Whitlock got in and drove off.

"How could you?" I smelled his drift.

"How could I what?" she asked.

"Associate with that Robert Chambers...that Joel Rifkin...that no good Buttafuoco." I plunged up all the slime of the age. "He's sleaze and strangle, he's..."

"He picks up his phone. I've been trying to call you every day for the past week since you were on that horrible stage, and your phone just rang and rang. I felt very depressed about what I saw. I liked you."

"I liked you, too..." I began.

"He came up to me at work and said he was your best buddy, and told me that you had a girlfriend and behaved that way because you were embarrassed to see me."

"He said that?!"

"I felt like such an idiot. I felt like I had been dumped."

"I'm sorry, but he was pestering me with phone calls so I had to…"

"Over the course of the week," she interrupted, "he consoled me. The Dean even let me take the day off."

"What?"

"Last night, he took me out for dinner, and we had some drinks, but even then I tried to call you. As usual, your phone just rang. I didn't know what to think."

"Honey," I said, and reached over to impart affection. Wham! She gave me a karate chop to my xiphoid process.

"Don't touch me again! I was in the Israeli army!"

"I was trying to comfort you," I said through gasps of pain.

"Yeah, by bargaining your way into my pants." As she left, I thought, there goes the only girl who ever really knew me well enough to not have anything to do with me. And certainly the only one that ever treated me exactly as I should have been treated, not much better or worse.

CHAPTER FOUR
WHEN CABS COLLIDE

I f you can't kill a mad dog, train and domesticate him. That apparently was the Whitlock policy. I felt like an Arab shopkeeper on the West bank, a Catholic merchant in Northern Ireland, a performance artist with an NEA grant.

At first I didn't take the proofreading job Whitlock offered, but after several weeks went by, I found myself sinking into debt. Finally, I broke down and called the number he had given me. I was immediately employed as a freelance proof-reader. This essentially entailed reading particular legal documents, comparing them with their prototypes, and making sure that the slight variations from one draft were carried over to the other. Soon enough, things became comfortable. The days fell like dominos.

Other than spending some of my newly-earned salary check furnishing my apartment, there was little excitement or deviation from monotony, until the day that she stole my heart.

* * *

After two months of working at the firm of Reigert & Mortimer, I became fascinated by her. Although she was a young associate, she was already on her way to being the youngest partner in the firm's history. What was this magical gift of hers? Negotiation. She was regarded as the Rambo of negotiators.

When a deal became thick with qualifiers, proxy battlers, options, offers, proposals, alternatives of all varieties, and the vision blurred as to which direction was forward, she'd be called in to commandeer the Big Push. She'd research an issue from every side, refine the corporate strategy, anticipate opponents and obstacles, figure how to handle different personalities, when to advance, when to retreat, but always to a victory. I would hear her from adjacent rooms; proofread documents that she had just thrashed out; see her passing in corridors flanked by aides, aerobicized in arguments.

Although I could never confess it to her, I was mercilessly in love (adversarial polarity). I would find exceptionally minute and fine-point ways of individualizing myself in her mind: lingering a moment longer than most when asked to give her some statistic or interest rate, paper-clipping a document at an arrogant angle, clearing my throat when encased with her in silence on a packed elevator. Perhaps it was all unnecessary. She might have recognized me because I was everything she wasn't: she was gorgeous, I left much to be desired; she was healthy, I was prone; she was youthful and tight-skinned, I was prematurely aged by excessive worry; she was snow white in the winter and tandoori tanned in the summer, I was perennially jaundice-yellow due to mushroom-like habits (not to mention loose and hairy skin— likely due to sedentary habits and fast foods); she was rich, I unrich; she had meaning, value, importance, was well-dressed, sweetly fragranced, sensual, yea-saying, clear-thinking, impeccable in periodontal care, incapable of shooting a political misleader, certainly unable ever to be rounded up as either a homeless person or an illegal alien…I… well, I've had problems in those areas.

Anyway, one night during the strung-out, final forty-first hour of an exceptionally long shift when I was all wired and frazzled, while slugging my umpteenth debenture, I noticed a complicated and abstract pattern of recurrent letters beginning each of the words on the left margin. The Cabala had convinced me that there were no such things as accidents (although the Koran implies it's all an accident). It was one of those White Album-esque kind of patterns that, in logical terms, I might be able to explain to maybe just a couple of geeks, or savants like Bobby Fisher, Alan Turing, or Stephen Hawkings. I carefully jotted down this obscure letter pattern. Upon arriving home that night, instead of showering in sleep, I downed about a quart of coffee and remained awake for an additional fifteen hours, poring over some deservedly rare books, piecing together a code. I erected a complex theory around the belief that Amy was trying to make contact. But she wanted proof of high intelligence, so I held on tight to that clerical Excalibur, trying to wrestle it from the rhetorical stone. The only man for her would notice this obscure code mummified in dead languages. He'd translate it as some kind of RSVP. The message I finally deciphered out of the code was approximate. Conjunctions and prepositions were inserted. It went: "Cupcakes of mid-November, voluminous looms of flying zinc and Betty..." It went on. In retrospect, I needed more time.

In prospect, though, it didn't matter. She'd recognize the effort. By the time I got that far, I realized that she was probably at her desk. She had recently returned from a big business deal in Europe, and I decided to use that as a springboard for conversation. Dialing her extension, I listened to her repeat hiccups of hyper hellos.

"Hi, this is Joseph." I carefully read her the encrypted "Cupcakes" message that I had decoded. She hung up. I called her back and tried a different approach.

"Hi, this is Joseph. I deciphered your code and decided to call you. How was your hop across the pond? Did you see the Louvre? I found Europe to be overrun with an American merchandising mono-culture that smothers the flavor of the locals. We're no longer the land of great trees, no sir. Franchises. Trademarks everywhere. You're corporate, am I right? So am I. We're not Americans. We're corporate. See my point? And now over there. In Greece, for instance, I couldn't find a single guy in a white skirt. In Italy, not a single Renaissancian figure. The Common Market is just another lame attempt at annihilating locality. Corporate consolidation is just a commercial attempt at old fashion Bukharin collectivizing, which we so roundly condemned in the…"

"Who is this?"

"Joseph, the proofreader. I deciphered your cryptogram. Did you get to southern Europe? I find the people to be less educated but truer to life, more sensual, uncircumcised, single-seasoned. Hello, Dionysus! And the economy is more inclined toward barter. Whereas, in the north, the earth seems more paved, but the people all seem to speak flawless English. Well, that's not true, but the girls are more repressed, hairless, and…"

"Who is this?"

"Joe. Remember, I passed you in the hall of Reigert & Mortimer? How long were you in Europe? Hey! What's the exchange rate? In 1980, there were six francs to the dollar, four hundred lire to the dollar, twelve pesetas to the dollar, two hundred drachmas…"

"Who is this?!" her voice roared with education, command, Napoleonic destiny. What a lady!

"Joseph, the proofreader. Were you in Amsterdam or…"

"Did Bart put you up to this?"

"Who?"

"What do you look like?"

"Kind of a cross between Jim Morrison and Val Kilmer…"

"I notice bodies, not faces."

"I'm medium height, I have a husky frame."

"Medium height. What's that, five-feet-eleven?"

"Well…not quite."

"What's your height and weight?"

"In America, don't you agree that they place way too much emphasis on standardization and externals? I mean, life is an automatic process. We're born and we go through the assembly line. Our days are given and automated. But we were once people of the valley without the valley, no? People of the mountain without the mountains, no? People of the…"

"Weight and Height?!"

"I really don't know. Economy size, if I must be marketed."

"In short, you're short…Weight!"

"Let's put it this way, whenever I sit on one of those orange, scooped-out subway seats, my cheek climbs over the side into the next seat. Those seats don't even have drainage holes. If someone urinates in them…"

"I remember you—the chubby dwarf."

"That's not technically true. There's a precise anatomical definition for a dwarf regarding the limbs-to-torso ratio—a definition that I exceed by ounces and inches."

"Okay, you're short and fat. Hold on, I got another call." She pushed the red, putting my life on hold.

What a broad! What pursuit of unbridled honesty! Now I wouldn't have to wear the corset or the lifts in my shoes. But more important, she cut right through the fat into the bone; she thought like an obnoxious male. She probably had a slide rule or something that could calculate the size of a man's reagan by just listening to the tone of his voice. In another moment, she was back on the phone speaking:

"You're Joseph Aeiou. You're twenty-three years old. You live a lonely life in a two-bedroom apartment on the upper East Side. You graduated Columbia on a Knights of Pythias scholarship, dropped out of an exclusive masters program to pursue a career as a stand-up comic."

"That's not entirely true." Whitlock had taken some liberties filling out my employment history, but I didn't want to identify him and this whole falcon-and-falconer relationship we were having.

"You've been a mediocre proofreader for several months now."

"Facts shade the truth!"

"You probably drink a lot of coffee and beer, have a lot of books and records, take a lot of drugs, compulsively masturbate, TV always on…"

"Let me remind you that Hugh Hefner was a twenty-seven-year-old using his kitchen table as a desk when he put out his first historic issue, which…"

"That's how you see yourself, isn't it?" she said knowingly.

"Actually, no." Although I presumed I had the same sleaze-capacity as Hef, I lacked the slick veneer. I was more of an Al Goldstein type.

"I'm curious about your apartment." She brushed me aside and took off. I had fumbled the puck, and now she was skating with it. "Do you live in a railroad flat?"

"No, I have two large bedrooms…"

"Tell me about the floors in your bedrooms."

"The floors?"

"What are they made of?"

"Wood."

"Buckled? Splintery? Lacquered?"

"Both are polished parquet."

"Tell me the measurements."

The apartment had been in my adoptive family for at least one generation. It was large, rent-controlled, and well-situated. I gave her more facts—about the recently installed crappy intercom that sucked in all the street noise, the fall-apart aluminum storm windows (a Mafia-landlord racket), and the width and height of door frames—and figures; I provided the average utility rates as well as the rate of increase per annum and the weight/stress ratio per square foot. I'd retained these housing details after getting stoned one day and deciding that I wanted to be a slumlord. But after a few hours, after coming down, I decided to be a warrior for the people, and then I got stoned again.

The rapidly fired questions unfolded into greater, more precise questions. We exchanged details faster and faster like machines until the pitch of our voices got insect-high. We abbreviated terms, more data per breathful, like seasoned catholics doing the rosary. At first, I sensed she was drawing a two-dimensional diagram. But as the questions got more minute, I realized it was lifting off the page into a three-dimensional model, complete with a small replica of me looking something like a demon spawn of the Pillsbury Doughboy and the Michelin Man. But it didn't really matter; I was utterly infatuated with that hot little voice. Looking down at my trusty reagan, I realized that I was in an achingly turgid state.

"Exactly what rent do you pay?"

"A hundred and twenty-eight fifty a month." I tied a tourniquet about my bobbing reagan to keep the little heathen still.

"Perfect! I'll be under the big brass clock in Grand Central at 5:30."

"The old four-faced clock on top of the Info Center?" I asked desperately.

"No, the big Merrill Lynch clock."

"But they removed that clock."

"Meet me under where it used to be. I commute from Westchester, but I've had it with commuting. In order to squeeze out more productivity hours, I need a place in the city." Suddenly, without a farewell, the line went dead. I thought maybe she'd hit the red button again, and was ingesting more facts on me. But after an eternity of holding the phone to my ear, a dial tone broke through.

I was pleased with the conversation. I really couldn't win her with my charm or accomplishments. The only strategy that ever really worked for me was pity. But never in the 250,000 years since the earth engendered homo sapiens had there been such a hot babe!

I got a little sleep, which after so many hours awake only

made me sleepier. I took a cold shower, had about a gallon of coffee, and sat on the toilet for around twenty minutes, without yield. Then I put on a new T-shirt which I'd won the last year from WFUK for being the eighty-fourth caller, and I played some records to get the decibel level of my confidence up. I emptied the stuff from my pockets that usually makes my pants droop. I had no roll-ons or aerosol crap, so I smeared some natural maple syrup on my neck and chest. It felt sticky, and I smelled like sap, but I realized I had no time for a shower.

I quickly went to the hiding place in the bathroom. I never had anything valuable but I was a great believer in hiding places and all their implications. When UFOs finally get around to squashing all mankind like bugs on their windshield and turning the earth into a big service station, if they fast-forward through the remains of our cultural history they might think—by our literature, arts, and music—that our planet was one great love-in. In point of fact, the gnarled imprint of guilt, shame, and distrust are on everything. The hiding place in the toilet underscored this. I only wished I could curl up in there. I took a twenty out of it, in case she wanted to go for drinks.

I squeezed into a rush hour subway. Three-and-a-half million people joined me. As we rode the number six to Forty-Second, we vied for seats and gripping bars. Like a dividing vacuum, whites exiting the subway were sucked into a pinpoint zero gravity center, apparently located somewhere in Grand Central. Blacks tended to stay on the subway.

Once up and out in that cathedral of commuters, I was locked in the density level of all these men in trench coats. I shoved until I could shove no more and, looking up between bobbing heads and entombing shoulders, I saw her. She seemed to be at the hub of a galaxy of people. She was truly statuesque. She seemed to be standing on a pedestal, a Goddess Diana in her modern-day temple of Ephesus.

Drones don't approach the queen. A small shell of space

surrounded her. With this advantage, she was able to survey the panic-stricken faces of trapped and orbiting commuters. Light seemed to be striking her at such an angle that it lent her a marble texture. I tried calling to her, but my voice couldn't compete with the din of the crowd; I tried waving to her, but my arms were wedged at my sides. Whenever I tried moving toward her, the crowd looped me further away. It was the spin-dry stage of rush hour. All I could do was stand there and wait until she spotted me. By that time I had to go to the bathroom something awful. All those people sucked the limited supply of oxygen. Others, somewhere on the outer edge of the city, were pushing in toward me. Everyone in the entire City of New York was at that moment contributing some inward pressure toward me.

The pounds per square centimeter on my rib cage and vital organs were immeasurable. Soon, I could hold no longer. I started farting incredibly. I literally felt as if I were deflating with flatulence: the odor of a million burning tires. Soon I started inhaling, gagging on my flatulence; I could feel that crap-gas filling my lungs, asphyxiating me! Businessmen started retching on the rising brown fog. A nucleation occurred.

After sitting stagnant for hours, stewing in acidically-reduced cold-cut sandwiches and pounds of slaw, my intestines must have resembled a two-ply garbage bag— the manswarm scrambled away from me at all costs. It was during this ripple in the crowd that enough of a space opened to individualize me. She looked down at the gap in the crowd and saw my wiggling shock of unwashed hair. She took giant steps, her stiletto heels seemed to be six feet tall. A giant Fay Wray seizing her chimp Kong, she rescued me to a place of calm.

"You're eight minutes late!" she yelled. "Do you know what my time is worth? Do you know what I would do to you if you worked for me?"

"I tried…I swear I tried…" It was difficult to speak, and I started hyperventilating as she continued yelling at me.

"Do you realize that because of you I will now be eight minutes late throughout my entire life. I'll never, ever be able to regain that lost time. You KILLED eight minutes of my life!" The crowd, the lack of sleep, the fact that the woman who I wanted to be mine—my lady—was infuriated with me—I was overwhelmed and I started weeping. Soon, it was uncontrollable.

"That's enough of that," she said, but I couldn't stop.

"That's more than enough of that!" But I only cried the more.

"That is quite ample," and, "here, here" and, "there, there" and, "that certainly fills the quota," all followed.

But I only cried the harder. It was all too much. A monsoon of coffee had burst the dam of my nerves, flooding me into a neurotic state. I started twitching and hiccupping through the tears. But the dam, as it turned out, had not completely broken until it happened. Both commuters and homeless alike watched in disbelief.

I involuntarily peed in my pants. A thick trickle ran down my right leg, along the marble floor, into a large, yellow puddle. It soon trailed off into some drain, connecting me to other bodies of foul waters.

She looked pityingly on me. "Every man I've met has been weak in some way…but you are the sniveling weakest." I sniffled more.

"Man is unrivaled," she proclaimed to an older group who had not evacuated the city in their mobile years and, by default, became native New Yorkers. "Man revels in weakness…." She paused; something must have clicked. I guess she extrapolated: Man equals weakness; I'm the weakest; ergo, I'm the most manly. I conclude this because of her next execution. She reached down, grabbed me, and pressed me so tightly against her breast that she actually lifted me about a foot off the ground. I felt like a saline implant. Rocking me back and forth, she started repeating over and over, "There, there," pause, "here, here."

I regained my composure slowly. Even though my feet couldn't reach the ground, my confidence was returning to me. Still whimpering so that she would continue holding me, I snaked my right hand carefully along the tight space between our bodies, gently placing the open palm against the invitation of her right breast, a da Vinci shape molded in heaven's own marble.

Dropping me, she emitted a high-pitched shriek that only dogs, I, and burly men who hate little people could hear. Pow! She whacked me with the back of her hand across my nose. Pow! A burly man who spends his life keeping an eye on little guys like me punched me deep in my stomach. Like a puck, I plopped to my hands and knees in pee. He kicked me in the stomach. Splash: goal! He disappeared into the crowd.

"Serves you right," she said as I gasped for breath, trying to prevent myself from vomiting. I could see drops of blood from my nose drip and disperse in the pond of urine.

"Now, let's see this apartment and get down to the nitty gritty," she said, and made her way out of the large building with the pretty ceiling. I couldn't believe that she could be attracted to me after that. I struggled to my feet and raced outside just in time to see her climb into a cab. Never had a woman—especially one in the presence of whom I'd lost my bladder control—wanted to just have me. I shoved in the taxi after her. She pushed into a corner, away from my salty dampness.

She wanted it bad. I wanted it bad. Apparently the cab driver wanted it bad, too, because he zoomed a hundred miles an hour to a red light five feet in front of us. In a moment the light changed, and the driver put the pedal to the metal.

"Where to?" the cabby inquired.

Feeling prosaic, I said: "To paraphrase E.B. White, I live twenty-two blocks from where Rudolph Valentino once lay in state, eight blocks from where Nathan Hale was executed, five blocks from where Hemingway punched out Max Eastman, four miles from where Whitman wrote editorials for the *Brooklyn Eagle*..." He screeched to a halt.

Because my arms were too short to brace myself against the front seat, and my legs didn't reach the floor, I fell into the leg area of the cab. She looked down at me and I smiled up at her meekly.

"Tell the chauffeur where we're going, you grinning idiot!"

I gave him my address as I tried to pry my waist loose from that dead zone. We moved like a high-speed checker piece, crisscrossing the bumpy board of Manhattan. The opponents were traffic lights, jay-walkers, and endless bike messengers who kept banging against the outer shell of our cab.

"We're not in a rush," I barked through the bullet holes in the Plexiglass divider.

"Time and tide wait for no man," the fanatic behind the wheel replied in broken English. I longed for the day that they empty Manhattan of all meddling pedestrians and make it strictly vehicular.

When we finally came to my place, the curb was on my side, the traffic on hers. She opened my door and shoved me out on my ass. Throwing a crumpled bill into the front seat, she stepped over me.

"Off the ground, mole, I've got an appointment in Westchester at 7:38."

I rose and huffed and puffed, trying to keep up with her. Each big step she took translated into a hundred little chihuahua steps for me. The fifty-plus hours of sleep deprivation were catching up with me. Sweat trickled down my brow. I was unable to concentrate or focus my pupils. It was like being in college all over again.

Finally, up some flights of stairs, we reached my floor. She threw open the door, shoving me out of the way, and stepped in. Taking it all in at once—the centerfolds on the wall, the large plastic garbage bags of undisposed trash, the stacks of books, the oddities, the curios, the knickknacks that I'd found in the street, and the light streaming along the columns of dust in the middle of the living room—she looked at me. I was very proud of my place. She silently walked around the apartment. Reaching into a box, she pulled out the brown bag that Whitlock gave to me containing my transcripts and other papers from my graduate program.

"What's hiding under this rock?" she muttered, and pulled out something I had never seen before—a copy of my birth certificate.

"Where did you find that?"

"You were born in Japan?" she asked, reading it. Looking under her shoulder, I saw that on some sundry vital statistic, under "Place of Birth," it said, Tokyo, Japan.

"I never knew that!" I replied.

Her response was a fit of gracious sneezes from her cute little nose. I located a slightly used napkin from the recesses of my pocket and offered it to her.

"This place is a pigsty." Sneeze.

"Judge not least ye be…"

"It's a filthy mess!" Sneeze.

"I don't deny that it can use some work. But a new broom sweeps clean."

"You need a new tractor." Sneeze, sneeze, sneeze.

"Come on in, I've got some Yodels and other Hostess pastries in the pantry…"

"I'm going to break out in hives if I stay here much longer. I'm allergic to this room." She retreated into the hall.

"Well, you cunt…"

"What?"

"Do you want to go to a motel or something?" I asked, hoping that she missed my slip.

"A motel? What in the world for?" she asked with a coy indignation.

"For the same purpose that we came here," I sneered.

She gave me an unusual look and replied, "There are no

high-ceilinged motels that I can rent in Midtown Manhattan for less than two hundred bucks a month, even with a simi- an sleazebag as a roommate." And then she began departing down the stairs.

"WHAT!" I said, after a momentary lapse into utter disbe- lief. I raced down the steps, catching her as she was hailing a cab on Third Avenue.

"I'll have to send some people over to help clear out my room, and then we'll need to sit down and draw up a sublease agreement. I might also bring in some carpenters to throw up some partition thing, maybe just a free-standing divider in the middle. I want you to call my office and tell my secre- tary when you'll be home. Do you understand?"

I automatically nodded yes.

"Are you going to forget?" I shook my head no.

"Damn, look at you. 'Course you'll forget." I promised her I wouldn't.

"I just need a place for two months until something else comes along. I'll return to you a renovated place and a year's rent. Fair enough?"

I automatically nodded yes again.

She hailed, and a cab screeched sideways to a halt. She got in, slammed the door behind her, and disappeared into that maze of moving metal that imperils the tortured people of this shaky city. Why in the hell would she want to live with me? She could buy and sell little people like me ten times over. What the hell was this all about?

With my last calories, I crawled up the stairs. Like some- one with diarrhea who can greet defecation by simply sitting on a toilet, I found sleep as soon as I got supine. But there was still no escaping the low-income sleep.

Many of my dreams and revelations came from the margins of the city, places like the subway or bombed-out, boarded-up brownstones, dank and populated with ill, foreign, ugly, hun- gry, poorly-clad people. Their laughs were nowhere near as powerful as their cries. They met their pleasures in perversity.

Their behavior was irrational, repetitious, erratic, tormenting, and I invariably awoke being chased. On this particular occasion, I dreamed I had just broken out of a large, leathery roach egg, and my father, a sewer rat named Drogun, was chasing me. I was at a perilous place on the food chain.

I awakened with a start, took a leak, ate a quart of Cherry Garcia ice cream, thought about the women's suffrage movement in the middle of the nineteenth century, disentangled my scrotum, and plunged back into that toxic gutter of muddy sleep.

CHAPTER FIVE

"WHOEVER SAID 'SIZE DOESN'T MATTER' WASN'T TALKING ABOUT NEW YORK APARTMENTS"

A nanosecond later, I awoke to the sound of something very heavy being dropped very near my head. I opened my eyes slowly. Amy and a couple of yuppies were rummaging around in the apartment. I went back to sleep. Later, I awoke to the sensation of having my bed hoisted up in the air and transported across the room. More yuppies filled the house. Every time I went back to sleep, I would awaken only more exhausted and drained. The next time I awoke, the place was packed with yuppies. I could see these were not the old yups of the early '80s, engendered by the false boom, who died out by the market correction of the late '80s. These were a deadly swarm of survivor yuppies who had mutated with New Democrats in the Clinton age. Their well-pressed lapels and jackets looked like wings. They were filling the place slowly and insidiously, like the crows in the jungle gym scene of Hitchcock's *The Birds*.

I tried to get up, but sleep was an obese bed-fellow, and I couldn't get out from under her. When I awoke for the last time, the lady of the house was there with only a few of them, the final nominees. They were all walking around inspecting details. It was like a competition of fastidiousness. She was talking to some guy with a tape measure and level. Most of my furnishings and belongings were now tightly packed into the rear third of the apartment, away from the healthy windows facing the street. My bed and I were firmly angled upon boxes. The other two-thirds of my apartment had all these idyllic things, like a prefabricated bar with a small statue of mercury and customized shelving. There were also several boxes of Ikea furniture waiting to be opened and assembled. A Port-O-San in the corner indicated that this was a union job.

They ignored me completely as I struggled to my feet and wrapped a sheet around my naked weight, searching for a grenade among my memorabilia.

"I have the lease in my name and I don't want any roommates," I said to one of them. But it was as if I wasn't there.

"Party's over, everyone out!" They ignored me. "Hey, what is this? I'm master of my castle, get out!"

"Can't you see we're talking?" Amy replied lividly. Grabbing me by the scruff of my loose, bulldog neck, she yanked me into the hall and pinned me against the wall.

"Yesterday, you said some things to me that no man ever said to me before."

"Did I?" I asked, wondering if she was pleased or angry with me.

"You seemed to care about me. You seemed to be the only man on this whole goddamned selfish island who… who…who was interested in my welfare."

"Well, sorry if I misled you, but you must make a lot of money. I'm sure you must find my assistance insulting."

"I didn't get to where I am today by accepting either apologies or buts. I've already accepted your offer, and if you fell down these stairs right now and broke your neck, that offer would be something that made you a much grander human being." To illustrate my humility, she leaned me perilously over the stairway.

"What offer was that?" I asked nervously.

"You said that if I get a carpenter to do a major renovation on your place, and make it presentable, and pay a year's rent, you would let me stay for two months. Now that's certainly not asking much, is it?"

I had no recollection of making any such offer, but two months wasn't a lengthy duration, and there seemed to be a decent profit in the deal. Man was cursed with a mental wattage that overlit the squalid sublet of his pointless life. That wattage turned good men into serial murderers, pedophilic stalkers, and assorted cult members. Drugs and booze were shades and tints designed to dim that needless beam of consciousness. Ergo, the rental windfall would provide me with beer, pot, and other cognitive rheostats for the entire year.

Additionally, some early morning—perhaps after a shower—her monogrammed towel might slip. At the end of it all, I could claim her hi-tech renovated place, with its saturno halogen lights and pastel-painted walls, a regular pleasure dome. I tried to orally accept her offer, but she said that for my protection she would take care of the legalities. We made an appointment to meet at an office where she would sign a sublease agreement. She didn't tell me the title of the firm, just the vaguely familiar address. It wasn't until I got to the rhombus-shaped building that my dread and suspicion were confirmed. It was Frankenstein's castle: Whitlock Incorporated.

When I asked the horse-eyed receptionist for Ms. Rapapport (Amy's last name), I assumed that some nerdy boyfriend was going to work out this sublet agreement. He was probably a specialist in corporate real estate who just happened to be working in the snake pit. When the Satanic Shah, Whitlock himself, appeared arm in arm with my little sublet roomie, my heart blew up like an M-80.

"What are you doing here?" Whitlock spat at me.

"This is Joseph, the roommate I told you about," she replied.

"Wait a second," I said to her. "Where did you meet this clown?"

"Be quiet!" he growled. "This is an office; people are making money." Turning toward Amy, he asked, "Is this some kind of set up?"

"I should be asking that!" I started.

"I gave him a break by letting him work as a proofreader after he tried to kill me," Whitlock revealed.

"Bullshit. The truth is you have a knack for finding girls I'm interested in and soiling them," I said, adding, "He doesn't practice safe sex."

He punched me suddenly in the gut. For a man his age, it was very powerful, knocking all the wind out of me. Grabbing my shoulder, Amy held me up.

"I'm sorry," she apologized to me for him—or vice versa.

"Now, Andrew, this is my affair. He has an apartment within my budget range. Remember who you are."

"Forget it," I piped in. "I'm not subletting to any friend of this guy."

"Come now!" she replied. "Enough of this. I want you two to shake hands."

"All right," Whitlock muttered, snatching my hand like a pickpocketed wallet.

"I actually thought we were kind of bonding for awhile back there," I replied as we shook.

"Good boys," she replied.

"This way," he said, and shoved me toward his war room. She trailed. His office was an agoraphobic's nightmare with the latest gadgets of fun and comfort. He instantly began pleading with her while I tried to catch my breath.

"For god's sake, Amy, let me buy you a place. You can pay me back whenever you want, but don't do this!"

I silently concurred.

"Sorry, Andrew, but I insist on autonomy."

"Then for Christ's sake, buy yourself a co-op," he pleaded. "Interest rates are nothing now. The real estate market has hit an all-time bottom."

"It's still too costly," she replied, "even for me."

He sighed the sigh of troubled love and mumbled something in the intercom to his horse-eyed secretary stabled outside. The door opened, and a lackey wheeled in a document; it was thick and written in fine print. In size it resembled the Treaty of Versailles. After she signed it, she handed me the document. Eager to just get out of there, I took out the Montblanc pen I had stolen from Whitlock earlier.

"My pen!" he exclaimed, snatching it from me. "That was given to me by the Prime Minister of Carraway, you thief." He handed me a Bic Ballpoint.

"So what am I signing here?" I thumbed through the document.

"A basic sublease agreement," said the well-pruned tyrant.

"A sublease agreement doesn't have to be the size of a phone book."

"Actually, that's a standard corporate real estate agreement there. Admittedly, my people made some modifications for this situation. If you like, take it home and look it over." I flipped through it quickly, a lot of party-of-the-first-part crap. It read like a Cartesian equation, an endless series of pointless statements and reasons.

"This looks like something from the foreign ministry. I'll get a standard Blumberg sublease that you can sign," I said to her.

"As a woman, I'm asking you to sign it." I'm not sure what sacred power being a woman carried, but I wasn't moved. It looked like a confession to the Lindbergh baby kidnapping.

"Come on, sign the damn thing, and let's get you the hell out of here," Whitlock yelled.

"I'm reluctant."

"Sign it, or I'll have you blacklisted from the proofreading circuit."

"Andrew, you won't do anything of the sort!"

"He already did something of the sort," I explained. "He had me expelled from college before I could drop out!"

"Well, he won't do it again," she said.

"He can't do it again. This is unfair. I didn't know he was your boyfriend."

"He's not," Amy exclaimed.

"Well, I still don't want to have anything to do with anyone who's a friend of his. You two deserve each other."

"What exactly happened between you two?" she asked Whitlock.

"Nothing at all. Joseph and I are best buddies," Whitlock said.

"This guy ruined me!" I countered. "He humiliated me, slept with Veronica…"

"Excuse us, Amy," Whitlock said, as he walked her to the door, "Me and Mr. Aeiou have some unfinished business to work out."

"No, we don't." I rose and headed out with her. I was afraid to be alone with him. He closed the door on her, and we were alone.

"Now, Aeiou, take it easy," he said, cracking his knuckles.

Whitlock went to a small refrigerator in a corner of his office and handed me a bottle of Heineken with a pubic hair on it.

"Fuck beer. You people come in here and think you can just take over. She makes more money in a day than I'll make in a lifetime. Why does she want my apartment?" The snake with a suit for skin took out a hundred dollar bill and extended it to me.

"A hundred dollars?! Who do I look like—Harpo Marx?"

While I protested, he took out a small vial of coke and the next month's issue of *Penthouse*, which hadn't yet hit the newsstands. Opening the pages, he put the magazine on the desk. Then on the edge of his desk he laid a long, thin line of coke. It looked like a fine strand of white hair.

"You cheapskate, that's the most paltry line of coke I've ever seen."

"It's pure," he said, handing me a gold-plated tube. I

hadn't gotten my share in the '80s, so I snorted it and…
"Ewwwww-weeeee!"

"There's more," he said. I remember popping things, pills and herbs and glasses of fine liquor with exotic larvae submerged at the bottom. He put something in my hand, and I signed a treaty to give Panama Canal back to the Lilliputians. And then I remember looking at 3-D nudes of women who screwed presidential candidates or ministers or chancellors or something. Porn from Cleopatra right on up. Pink dishwashing gloves turned inside out. And then Amy walked back in the room and thanked Whitlock and asked for my keys, which she returned a second later, saying that she had had them copied; another fine white line, and she was asking when to send two carpenters named Mason and Dixon to build an Iron Curtain down the middle of my apartment, with her on the Serbian side and me on the Croatian. I couldn't stop smiling, into the street, accelerating right into the middle of a million lives that I'd never know, launched through subway throngs for the rush hour, weaving like a wave runner, leaving all in my wake bobbing up and down. I wasn't going anywhere. It was just a pleasure cruise on the current of life, a scuba dive in the great ocean of mankind, feeling strange flesh—young and old, poor and middle class, hot and cold—pressed against mine. As the packed train stopped at Times Square, I developed a bizarre fear. Physicists have observed that when a big-ass star exhausts its nuclear fuel, it crushes together with such force that its gravity becomes inescapable. I kept finding myself at the center of this massive collapse, the black hole of this rush hour.

I had to prevent it or I'd be crushed into spaghetti. When the subway doors opened, people outside, free of manners, crushed inward. Those behind me, equally eager, pushed outward. The masses—I love 'em—they rush for red lights, risking everything to capture a few seconds, only to get home and waste their lives.

I threw my arms across the frames of the sliding subway doors and held on like Samson, not allowing any of the crushing commuters behind me, or any of the commuters in front of me, to pass—a Spartan at Thermopylae. Finally, when the big boom occurred, I popped out like a champagne cork, flying right into one of those big metal pillars. I had an ear bleed. When I got home, I sat down, fell asleep, woke up, and sat down again. I dreamt that I'd just signed away my apartment, my life, and lord knows what else.

CHAPTER SIX
RELAX, YOU'RE
SOAKING IN IT

I was frequently sick with both systemic contaminations and mechanical fractures. I have broken limbs eight times (but I haven't broken eight limbs). Sprains have been countless. Infections, both viral and bacterial, have been so frequent I have learned to function with them. I was a recognized face in the university health services office, and I popped a carousel of antibiotics because my bacterium would develop quick immunity. (The school nurse once tried to nickname me "Petri [Dish]," until I threatened her with a suit.) So it came as no surprise that the morning after the signing, to the sound of bumping and moaning, I awoke with a low-level fever and a sinus infection.

Amy was moving some boxes into my apartment with the help of her SWBs—Spry White Boys. They made the mistake of parking some boxes on the landing before hopping downstairs to the double-parked van to find a legitimate parking place. Quickly, I opened a box and fumbled through it for whatever dirt I could find. No topless beach photos or nights of photographic abandonment. The most interesting detail I could tweeze was a high school yearbook. I folded the box closed and took the album to my room. She graduated from Bismarck High, Bismarck, North Dakota. The Bismarck High Muskrats was the school's varsity team. The Bismarck

High Scream was the school paper. Finally, I located her picture. WOW!—Teeth like a rabbit. Eyes like a crow. Skin like a cobra. Flipping through the yearbook, I saw the nervous, humorless inscriptions of her freaky friends and checked out their vile visages. They were equally stilted and ingrown; runts of the litter, all.

Within the album were some recently snapped photographs, apparently from her tenth-year high school reunion. Group photos of the same old high school buddies revisited years later. In the same way that crappy apartments were renovated before their rents were inflated, her friends were now attractive. Details had been improved, hiding the structural flaws.

Mindlessly, I chewed on countless packets of sugar until my insulin level spiked and I started feeling incredibly light-headed. I was worried when I accidentally drooled on one of the pages of her yearbook, so I quickly placed it back in the box still in the hall. Feverishly, I recalled my high school era. I had gone from ugly to uglier over the years (which is both natural and healthy; after all, we die at the end). Yet I remembered the others—that bespectacled group that looked a lot like Amy's high school bunch.

As my temperature climbed, and the sinus infection migrated down my throat, I remembered something that had happened about a month ago while I was on a proofreading case. I was proofing a legal contract for a business located in Bismarck, North Dakota. An agricultural- research firm was filing for bankruptcy because a large tract of their land had somehow been contaminated due to a spill in a nearby chemical factory. Initially, I just assumed it was another radiation-waste debacle covered up by the Department of Energy.

A lawsuit was being handled by another firm, and I couldn't get access to the dirty details. A corporate disaster is usually messy business: exposures, large-scale worker dismissals, whistle-blowers, government investigations, heavy fines, new legislation—all of this seemed to be part of the recipe. Lawsuits pour in from all directions. Yet, it seemed perversely odd how this particular Bismarck occurrence went against the grain. No one was dismissed or even transferred. Except for this one meager suit from this agricultural company, no one else was suing (which struck me as unpatriotic). No extensive investigation, or even mock investigation, was being conducted. Instead of being defensive or apologetic, their official statements seemed pat, curt, artful.

Awakening from my delirium of recollection to the realization that I was burning up, I took a bath in freezing water to try and bring my temperature down. From the tub I made a phone call to the local newspaper in Bismarck. Claiming to be a fellow correspondent, I learned additional details. All residential houses in the area had been purchased and emptied *before* the alleged spill—as if the spill had been anticipated. The incident occurred a couple years ago, but the area was still inaccessible.

The one actual detail that confirmed the nature of my suspicions was that the chemical company, as well as the Jasper Agricultural Company, were both held by the Merlin Corporation, a holding company that had as its parent—you guessed it—Whitlock Incorporated.

Eventually, I came to a point where I realized that I could learn no more unless I made an informal, investigative trip to Bismarck. Unfortunately, one of my great character flaws was that I could only do something up to the point that it required true courage. Beyond that, at the vital moment when action was required, I usually ended up watching a lot of television. By early afternoon, the infection had tendrilled down into my lungs.

Too exhausted and tuned-out to rise, I found myself marooned in a chair before the TV, watching an old rerun of *Bewitched*. I slipped between dreams and delirium, drinking flat, old beer and eating some Yodels from yesteryear. Where'd we be without preservatives?

As Samantha and Darren interacted, I thought about

boarding a Greyhound bus. The ride would probably be hell. I daydreamed arriving in downtown Bismarck at eleven at night and hailing a cab. I envisioned the cab driver as looking like Larry, Darren's white-haired, white-mustached, ass-licking/ass-kicking boss. I told him to rush me over to the Jasper Agriculture fields. He looked at me oddly. "That's a long way away, stranger. How about a hotel until the sun comes up?"

"To the field I must go."

"But it's a six-hour drive," he whined. "There's a big cyclone fence around it."

"There's always a big cyclone fence! Look, either take me there or I'm getting out." (My dream self didn't take no for an answer.) I was about to open the car door. He gunned the engine and did what he did best—drove. It was a long and silent ride. The driver nervously tried locating a radio station, but we reached the point beyond all frequencies, just rolling fields of radiation. Finally, around 4:00 in the morning, we drove down a dirt road. There was a putrefying smell in the air. I knew I was near a great and macabre discovery. Soon we came to an empty field encircled in fencing. I gave Darren's boss a hundred dollar bill.

Wordlessly, he took it, slipped it into his shirt pocket, and, with a blank, bloodless expression, zoomed away from that splotch of melanoma on the face of the earth. I struggled over the large fence and held my nose as I wandered around on the empty lot. There was a spongy feel to the earth, not just loose soil. After walking a bit, I soon became aware that my feet were wet. My eyes started to drool and burn. In the blurry distance I could see the outline of a huge silo. Behind it was a roofed area; I headed toward it. It wasn't a building, just corrugated roof over a wall-less, empty frame that continued; stalls divided the space, but what the stalls were for wasn't apparent.

After an hour or so, I started wheezing. I took out a white, monogrammed handkerchief, snot-free, and covered my

mouth, intent on searching for whatever I could find. As the
first rays of dawn came up (although admittedly there was
never a sunset or night in my vision, just a sudden and brilliant dawn), I saw that a thick, purplish oil had soaked
through my white socks and the cuffs of my pastel-colored
pants. I was on a large field and was having increasing difficulty breathing. I realized, oddly, that I hadn't seen a thing
since I got there. There were no birds. No insects, nothing,
just silence, me, the unclotting earth, and Canada (which
happens to border North Dakota, a coincidence—probably).

Soon I was gasping for air. I realized that I had to get off
the land quickly. I started running. I tripped, and my hands
sank into the earth. When I pulled them out, they were covered with bloody oil. I started digging. After uncovering just
several inches of earth, I found it: decomposing flesh, small
patches and strips of it. Some of the fleshy patches had
strands of hair. I also located shards of bones. I put a sample
in my pants pocket and retraced my steps back to the dirt
road. No sign of Larry the Cabby.

It was around noon by the time I got over the fence, covered with dirt and blood and oil and death. I hitchhiked back
to the airport and took the next plane back to The City.
People stared at me indiscreetly, as if I had just given birth
in the plane's bathroom, but my secret would be greater than
that.

On the plane trip, I thought about the discovery. This was
not a mass grave. It was a disposal sight. I could imagine it
all. Somehow, one Walpurgisian night—probably foretold by
Nostradamus (who also mentioned that the world would fold
in 3097) and trance-channelers (many of whom were former
suburban housewives)—thousands of malformed high
school graduates from around the country had gathered
together. Perhaps in the same manner that Spock was able
to hear all his fellow Vulcans cry out as one before being
destroyed, they, too, heard each other's silent screams. They
met under the corrugated roofs of the large empty barns,

where only fields of hay surrounded them for miles; they gathered and vaguely recognized each other. Lugubrious, obsequious, they had seen each other for years, in hallways, lingering around doorways, at the optometrist, at the orthodontist, in all types of waiting rooms, waiting to have their bite and sight corrected. They slowly touched each other's sores and lacerations. Rubbing their spindly bones and bad backs. They noticed the rope burns on their emotional wrists, extension-cord lashes on their misunderstood backs, and saw their asymmetrical faces covered with problematic and combination skin (dry *and* oily).

I could envision what occurred. Time was divided into long, arduous tactical conferences and strategy symposiums. They spent the night building, tinkering, hammering, and decimating.

I'm not saying this happened recently, or even ten years ago. (Maybe it only happened metaphorically.) It is foreseeable that they waited through the morass of Carter's moralism and the last of the cumbersome disco age, a time of domestic polyester and third-world bullies: Ethiopia, Libya, Vietnam, and Iran.

(The '70s were basically a visionless duration. At best, it was the rear guard of the '60s. Vietnam was lost and won. Former prophets were making a profit. Movements stopped moving, folk singer Phil Ochs had committed suicide. But the '80s!)

They had the perseverance of a cult, the investment strategies, and their parents' hard, cold cash, but they realized that their tell-tale signs would give them away. The porous skin, the Chia Pet scalps or Hitlerian bangs, the freakish manners of laughter—all these had to be well camouflaged. Enviously, they had learned that good looks were a membership card to anywhere. That very night, the experts in the crowds set up booths in the massive barn. There were mass facial dermabrasions and contemporary haircuts. Radical weight-loss and weight-gain programs were initiated.

Teams of plastic surgeons worked around the clock. Piles of oily flesh and hair had to be buried in the outlying hay fields.

After the transformation was complete, everyone was probably issued a wardrobe: a perfectly tailored suit, a shirt, a tie, shoes, and a briefcase filled with a dossier and a directive. They were never to acknowledge each other should they meet. And off they went.

In a conspiratorial silence, they attacked the early '80s, an army of ants decimating a plush forest, digesting trees, from leaves to roots, leaving only stones and bleached bones behind.

Where was this leading to?

In small-town squares, cob-webbed bells had to be located and rung! Red buttons had to be pushed! Phones had to be picked up! Senator Proxmire had *Mein Kampf* translated into English in the mid-'30s to warn America of the monster they were about to confront. Then another Senator flashed in my head: a paper being waved by McCarthy, February 9, 1950, before a Republican women's club in Wheeling, West Virginia. The buffoon speaks: "I have in my hand a list of two hundred and five names that were...members of the Communist Party...and are still making and shaping the policy of the State Department." I would have to spend the night drawing up notes and plans, outlining an exposé on this movement, comparing it with other cataclysmic movements. I was the Quasimodo under this bell!

As the plane was about to land in Kennedy Airport, I went up the aisle to tell the plane full of people what I had learned. I reached into my pocket for the fistful of putrid flesh...the pocket was empty.

In fact, I wasn't wearing pants. I was sitting naked in front of the TV. I no longer had a reason to lounge around in that warm mud-bath of an illness; the fever had broken. I took a leak and ate a brick of cream cheese that I found in the fridge. Then I began masturbating to the sexual testimonials on that afternoon's various talk shows. I fell asleep, hand on knob, before the end.

The carpenters came the next morning, and I watched as they referred to a blueprint that Amy and Albert Speer, Jr. had drawn up. They ripped out the walls, floor, and ceiling until the front half of the building was raw brick and joists. Then they started building. A plumber channeled off pipes and laid in a deep, terra cotta tub. Electricians rewired the place. A new wall shot up from the exact line of where her property began and mine ended. Once that wall was erected, I could no longer see a thing. That small, sacred sanctum that once contained my bed-box now held her toilet bowl. Sleepy, soothing, sedative colors were painted around her room.

My apartment was subdivided and under foreign occupation. For all I knew, they were assembling a big Panzer tank behind that partition, pointing it squarely at my room. Why was I going along with all of this? Because of a cockroach crawling around in the bloody chambers and tubes, impossible to squish dead. That cockroach was love—adversarial polarity—for her.

What is adversarial polarity all about?

Because no one is singular, no feeling is permanent, and no standardized definitions of emotion can exist, there can be no such thing as LOVE. Along with God and patriotism, love is just another great marketing tool. However, there is adversarial polarization, or a.p. Using the cold war as a paradigm, I had devised a realistic form of a relationship, in which two people of equal power were naturally balanced in wit and passion, with virtually equal doses of lust and distrust, the forces that attract and dispel. And therefore, through careful diplomacy, with checks and balances, there can be a lasting *détente*, a peaceful coexistence. This was adversarial polarity.

When feeling neurotic, I behaved unusually. In the same way that some people chew gum, gnaw fingernails, or smoke,

I tried getting channels on VHF that didn't exist. I whipped open the window and tried catching the masses in the street off guard, testing my theory that all reality was a God-made illusion designed to deceive me, and me alone, that mankind was static, like mannequins, until I was in its presence. Finally, I dialed what seemed like thousands of phone numbers, hanging up after the first ring. I dialed until the last knuckle of my index finger was sore and swollen. (Who knows what mass hysteria or paranoid effects I might've caused?)

A soft knock—I pulled on my pants and tossed open the door. There was She. I was dead at the knees and red in the face, riled and beguiled.

"Those animals you hired, they truncated my apartment," I established.

"You're embellishing."

"They bullied me and made me feel small and inferior," I clawed.

"You are small and inferior," she clarified.

"They made me feel even smaller and inferior-er."

"I'll talk to them. In fact..." She disappeared mid-sentence into the hall to go through the new and separate entrance to her apartment.

"And don't play the radio too loud!" I screamed because that was all I could think of. But as soon as I took my clothes off—there's no reason to be dressed when alone—my unlocked door opened wide again, and there she was, with a complete construction crew, eight large Italians, all of them standing there, staring at my sun-dried reagan.

"Hey, doesn't anybody knock around here?"

"For a bossy guy, you sure got a teensy set of nuts," the contractor said as I covered my privates.

"This is Fleming." She introduced him, ignoring his comment. "He's my resident carpenter. He'll be working here for some time, and it'd be nice if you could make an effort to be friendly to him."

"But I thought he was finished."

"He'll be working here for some time; I thought I made that clear."

Here, now, were my thoughts and subsequent words: Wasn't this absurd? "This is absurd!" Why should I have to put up with this? "I don't have to put up with this!" Didn't I enjoy living alone? "I enjoyed living alone!" How did all this happen? All I ever really wanted was to unclip those garter belts from those black fishnet stockings, pull down those flimsy, white-lace panties with the rip-away velcro crotch, and smell her fragrance: "All I ever really wanted was a little scratch and sniff!"

"What?" the resident carpenter exclaimed, locking me in a full nelson. One of his buddy boys turned his power-tool arms loose on my looseness.

"Stop that at once!" Amy commanded, after they had only severely damaged my large intestine.

"I want…you out…of here," I said to her, through tears of tearing pain.

The guy grabbed me back in a half nelson this time. I guess he was only half as angry. The other guy grabbed my face, putty in his palm.

"Release his face!" she called out. He did.

"I'm sure we can work this out," said the feminine voice of civility, as I re-sculpted my nose.

"Why don't you let us 'talk' to him a minute," the resident carpenter offered. "I think we can 'talk' man to man."

"I think everything's all right," she replied.

And they all went back into her part of the house where I could hear them demolishing with laughter. I quickly dressed and went to Landlord-Tenant Court at 110 Centre Street, where I filed a case on the docket. I, too, could play hardball.

For the next couple of days I put up with the constant racket. I put up with construction workers kicking my door when they went by. I put up with loud, nasty comments like,

"He must be scared of elephants 'cause he's got a peanut between his legs." I put up with it all because I knew I'd have the last laugh.

In a week or so, the carpentry stopped. They had finished whatever it was they were building. A couple more days went by and I got a notice in the mail to appear in Landlord-Tenant Court, which meant she'd received her notice as well. I laughed that morning as I read the notice. The trump was mine, but just to impart the final knee to the groin, I unscrewed the fuses in my apartment. The electricians might have rewired her place, but there was still only the one fuse box, and it was in my room. I also turned off all the water valves. The siege was on!

I spent the day feeling pretty good about myself and others. It was a great day, warm and sunny, so I went to the movies—*Home Alone 2*. I walked around—up Wall Street. I subwayed to a big indoor mall—the Trump building. I bumped into an old boyhood chum—Critter. Ate a fish dinner—sole. Finally I returned—home. She had broken into my apartment and turned on everything I'd turned off.

I ran into the hall and banged on her door. "You fucking bitch, I'm going to kill you, do you hear me!"

"Please don't," she yelled back in a calm voice, "I'm sure we can talk about things reasonably."

"Fuck reason! Open this door, I'm going to kill you!" I continued pounding and screaming until about a half an hour passed. At that time a duet of cops appeared behind me; I was about to explain my woes when suddenly she came out.

"She took half my apartment from me! Now she's trying to take the remainder!" Some high-strung rookie walked me into my apartment, and the ethnic, virile, senior partner who resembled the deceased actor Vince Edwards (TV's *Ben Casey*) disappeared into her apartment.

"Okay pal, what's up?"

Slowly and calmly I started to explain my story. But spotting my collection of rare issues of *Hustler* in cardboard boxes, he apparently played a hunch.

As I explained the underside of my story, he fingered through the fused-together issues that I had had to stack rather hastily. Suddenly, just as I was getting to the part where Amy's thugs had damaged my duodenum…

"What the fuck is this!" he exclaimed, pulling out a nickel bag of old and shitty grass.

"I never saw it before!" Always deny.

He twisted my arm around and shoved me face forward against the wall. In a single, well-practiced motion, he whipped his handcuffs around my wrists.

"She planted it!"

I remembered purchasing it one desperate night on First Avenue and Ninth Street and had never even bothered to smoke it. Usually I put whatever drugs I had in the hiding space under the toilet. He dug through all my belongings, which he tossed into a pile. Although he didn't find any more drugs, he did scrounge around boxes until he located my head-shop collection: bongs, metal pipes, rolling paper, and so forth.

By the time the high-strung rookie finished reading me my rights, my door opened and in entered the virile fuzz checking his zipper.

"This guy's a dope dealer. What'd you find out?"

"This scumbag subleased half the apartment to this lady at an exorbitant rate, and no sooner did she move in then he started hitting on her, threatening her with eviction unless she consented to oral-genital sex."

They pushed me roughly down the stairs. Several times I almost lost my footing. Into the back of a squad car I was shoved, again falling sideways into that familiar leg area.

We ended up at a Kafkaesque locale called Manhattan Central Booking. They took fingerprints and mug shots of me, then they sat me at a desk in front of a detective who looked exactly like the late actor Lee J. Cobbs.

"Occupation?"

"Politico-social historian in the epic tradition."

"Unemployed," he concluded, and typed it in with opposing index fingers.

He then asked me to sign a confession to my alleged crime. He also said that if I wanted to confess to the charge of coercing sodomy (Fellatio is legally termed as sodomy!), it would be better in the long run. Like Roman Catholicism, the more I confessed now, the easier it would be for me later. Indeed, if I were planning future crimes, I could confess to them as well. I informed him that I wasn't read my rights, this was an illegal arrest, and added, "Unless I'm given an apology and driven home this instant, I will notify Geraldo Rivera, Howard Stern, and Rush Limbaugh."

He led me to a public phone and said, "Call." I called information but felt too embarrassed to ask for the numbers of Geraldo, Howard, or Rush. I thought of calling some friends, but I didn't know their numbers and I knew they'd all be unlisted if not entirely disconnected. Nervously, I dialed some random numbers and hung up after the first ring. Someone finally picked up before the ring ended, and I lost my quarter. Since I had no outstanding warrants, I assumed I would be released on my own recognizance.

I was taken to an empty cell that smelled like dead pigeons, but soon it started filling up. My fellow inmates were holding their bruised heads and talking reminiscently.

"What you in for?" I finally employed the cliché.

"We were just fucking around, minding our fucking business in Tompkins Square Park, and next thing we know, the fucking pigs are clubbing us and then fucking tossing us into paddy wagons."

"Fuck!" I replied in unity.

Others, the latest characters from the Tompkins Square saga, joined us and exchanged their tales of woe, employing "fucking" not merely as adjectives and adverbs but also as prepositions, pronouns, and conjunctions.

Convicted felon Leona Helmsley—the Eva Braun of New York real estate—was not incarcerated in that particular cell. That particular cell was loaded with white anarchists, downtrodden black and Puerto Rican guys, all foreigners in their own country, fellow sublets who had been rounded up on this latter-day *Kristallnacht*.

Sleepily, I sat in a corner, suppressed tears, and wondered if they would deport me to the unknown land of my forefathers. I soon fell into a nauseous sleep. A lurid, vivid, tumultuous dream, which included the background sounds of the jail, encircled me: Riker's Island was vastly overcrowded, and so were the Staten Island ferries. All of them were jampacked with prisoners. Finally they sealed all the exits and filled the subways with convicts. As I walked through the city streets, fingers of the prisoners protruded, squirming through the subway grates and even cracks in the sidewalk. They were begging and moaning for anything. Sometimes they were spat on, and sometimes hard shoes would walk on the grill, crunching down on their fingers like snails on a moist suburban morning.

I was awakened to find a cop was shaking me. He told me to follow him. He led me to a desk where I was informed that I had no outstanding convictions and that the lab had determined that my grass was 100 percent catnip. Regarding the allegations of sexual coercion, the young lady had refused to press charges. In short, and much to their chagrin, I could go.

When I got home I couldn't believe what had happened. Somehow, she had entered my apartment and had switched the fuse box and water mains to her half of the house. An intensive, extensive job in electricity and plumbing had been done in a matter of hours while I was in jail. I sat on the ground among the rubble caused by the quick construction, only to be awakened in a couple hours when the phone rang. Someone claiming to be a representative from my proofreading agency said, "Aeiou, how do you spell compassion? Don't answer that; you might spell Rolaids. I just got a call from

Reigert & Mortimer. Someone said you mis-spelled the word once too often and, unless you're thrown to the winds, they're pulling the account. Well I got news, ta ta..." Click.

In the five thousand years of recorded history, had there yet been a legal document with the word "compassion" in it?

Amy had put the wooden stake through the heart. She had not only gotten me fired, she had trumped up the charge that I was unable to spell the word "compassion." What a diabolical sense of the acerbic!

Ironically (since I was just released from jail for not having pot), I retrieved my actual cache of pot from under the toilet and lit up to calm down. I also took out a line of acid drop papers that had the words "12-step program time" printed on them. Why? Why not?

I leaned against that wall dividing me from her and busily smoked a joint, trying to get over the loss of my crap-ass job.

Suddenly, though, I thought I felt an optic nerve pinch, but no! It moved! The wall! Just about a sixty-fourth-of-an-inch, but it actually moved into my half of the apartment. I stared at it some more, and through pin pricks of light I could see it recede backward. No longer trusting myself, I got my camera and patiently lay in wait for the beast to show itself. All the time, I wondered what the hell was going on. Was it an optical illusion? I touched the wall. It felt like half-inch drywall sections innocently anchored into aluminum studs, nonchalantly secured to joists—a very shrewd camouflage. I drew pencil lines along the points where the wall met the other walls, the ceiling, and the floor. After two hours, I did more acid to keep from falling asleep, and that's when I saw it pulsate again. It only did it for a second, but I was able to snap the picture. The first thing next morning I took it to the Fotomat.

I waited.

Twenty-four hours later I got the film back. In the interim, when I came down, I figured it was all an illusion. My perception must have been twisted by the chemicals in my brain. But one little item changed all that. In one of the photos there was a slight blur in the upper half of the wall. Evidence of motion could be clearly detected. Regarding my case, I considered all my charges against her. First, she had made me sign a contract under pharmaceutical duress. But that would be my word against hers. To give me the edge of credibility, I quickly urinated into an empty Styrofoam cup that formerly held that morning's coffee. The judge, if he so deemed, could analyze the metabolites (or whatever they were) in my specimen. After years of drug saturation, not to mention the joint I had just smoked, I was sure I would still turn up proof-positive, showing that any contract I ever signed had not been lucidly agreed to.

I also wanted to bring up the fact that she had her workmen intimidate me, but I had no witnesses, no bruises. She had had the water and electrical mains rerouted through her room; that was indisputable. But the "wall picture," my Exhibit A, made me confident that I could win the case. The cup of urine, too, would be a help, but just to be safe, I spent the evening toking grass and blowing smoke bubbles in the piss through a straw.

CHAPTER SEVEN
ROACH MOTELS & GLUE TRAPS

L& T, 110 Centre Street: Unprecedentedly, I was early. I entered and took a seat in a room that resembled a large storefront church. On the far side of what looked like an altar were the judge and his uniformed, overweight stooges. On my side were the pews, filled with angry and misshaped parishioners. I didn't see Amy. With my cup of urine in one hand, a book in the other, I was an excerpt of *savoir faire*. I squeezed into a seat. Because my last name began with an "A," my case would be on top of the cattle call. Reading Arthur Nersesian's self-published classic, *The Fuck-Up*, I quickly heard the court crier cry, "AEIOU vs. RAPAPPORT." His twisted pronunciation of my name sounded like, "Hey you!" and every twit in the place simultaneously pointed at himself and asked quietly, "Me?"

As I approached the bench, all the while looking for her, I bumped into some hyperactive post-adolescent who was carefully balancing a cup of soda. Perhaps it was his liquid Exhibit A. Of course it spilled all over me. The liquid had an acrid aroma to it. The kid raced off as if he had stolen my valuables, and the yeller yelled my name again.

"I'm Aeiou," I said, trying to wipe the smelly stuff off my relatively good clothes. "Do I win by default?"

"We're Rapapport," I heard sung in harmony behind me. I

turned around to see them: Four well-suited young lawyers, each armed with a briefcase, were casting a long, collective shadow over me. Amy was safely in the middle of them. It was like a Secret Service phalanx guarding their presidette. Whatever legal pyrotechnics they might have in their brief-cases couldn't rival the fact that I was right.

"Room six," the head clerk announced. We all marched off to room six. A small room with two tables and six chairs was where justice would be meted out. A balding, older, over-weight guy with an incredible goiter was the judge. As he mumbled some formalities and then read some forms, I couldn't take my eyes off that enigmatic growth on his neck. It seemed to beckon me. Since I had brought the com-plaint, he asked me casually, "What's on your chest?"

"Firstly, Miss Rapapport," I pointed to her, "connived a lease out of me. Secondly, she divided my apartment in half. Thirdly, she has been moving the wall closer and closer into my part of the house, and the thing is, her yuppie friends have been conspiring to destroy my life. She also got me fired from my job for mis-spelling the word 'compassion' and…"

"No, no, what's on your chest?" He pointed to my chest. My shirt and pants were filled with holes large and small.

"What's that smell?" the judge sniffed. "It smells like bat-tery acid or something."

"They did it!" I hollered. The post-adolescent who'd spilled what I thought was soda must have been an agent of theirs. "They did it! She! See, I'm one of the normal people and she's…"

"Enough! Prove it."

"No problem." Confidently, I held up the Styrofoam cup of urine and pulled out my photo and put it before him.

"It looks like a photo of a wall."

"Isn't it brilliant? The subtlety of it! Isn't it just genius?"

"What the hell are you talking about?"

"Examine, if you would, the top left hand corner of the photo."

"Yeah, so?"

"The wall is moving! The wall moved! She did something to make the wall move! She made the damned wall move. Her and those warlock workmen. This is indisputable."

"No, it's not. You could have moved the camera when you shot this photo. What other proof do you have?"

"This," I said. He held out his hand and I handed him the cup. He sniffed it deeply.

"What is it?" he asked.

"My pee."

He put the cup down and wiped his hand off carefully while I elaborated. "She drugged me, and cocaine-positive metabolites are in that vessel."

"What other proof?"

"What else?!" Distraught, in disbelief, and dissed, I despaired and felt panicky. I soothed my anxieties by stepping a bit closer to the radiance of his glowing goiter. I knew if worse came to worst I could somehow appeal to the humility of his goiter.

"We'd like to state our defense," they said in chorus.

"Go on."

"Wait a second," I said to the goiter. "May I approach the bench?"

"I don't have a bench."

"Can I whisper in your goit…ear?"

"My ear?"

"It's urgent!"

"All right," said the judge with some resignation.

I had no idea what I was going to say but I had to make it clear to him what was going on. I leaned over his goiter. It looked like a dinosaur egg. I smelled it. It didn't really smell. It had streaks and colors running through it that seemed to be a great amalgam of mystery. It was kind of a great unification.

"Well?"

"Did you ever see *The Invasion of the Body Snatchers?*" I said in a whisper.

"The film with that tall British actor with the mustache…"

"Whose son cheated on Julia Roberts…"

"Yeah, Donald Sutherland!" he said.

"He's actually from Canada, that's the remake."

"Well, that's the only one I saw."

"That's all right. Remember how pods from a foreign planet come to earth and replicate bodies of Earthlings…"

"What's your point, son?"

"These people in front of us, look at them."

"So?"

"They're yuppies, right?"

"I suppose so," he replied.

"Well, are they yuppies or not? Please correct me if I'm wrong."

"Yes," he conceded. "So what?"

"Where were they ten years ago?"

"I haven't the foggiest," he replied, and added, "If you've got something to tell me, you'd better tell it now because I'm all out of patience."

"They're from somewhere else—Bismarck, North Dakota. And they're trying to peel us away. They lure us. They draw us out into their glue traps and then they drown us while we're stuck there struggling and squealing…"

"I want to help you but…"

"Look, I can tell you're one of me. Together we can take back all those goddamned buildings that they changed into their bases."

"What bases?"

"You know, all those massive co-ops named after Midwestern states or Waspish names. The places that these guys had to bribe in order to get around all the local zoning ordinances and are built on New York landmarks!"

"Huh?"

"We can rebuild Penn Station and Moondog and the Third Avenue El and…it's culture-cleansing!" I screamed.

"Were you born in this city? Is that it?"

"No, but…"

"Were you raised in the city?"

"No, but…"

"Well, then, what are you talking about?"

"They're with the Mafia," I finally said.

"The Mafia?!"

"One of them," I muttered, stepping up closer.

"Which of these people," he pointed to the group, "are with the Mafia?"

"No, I mean they are each with one of the many mafias."

"And how many mafias are there?"

"More than I could ever count."

"Look," he exhaled slowly and, looking over to Amy's band of thieves, said, "I see what appear to be four very expensive lawyers over there. And I see you all alone. In trying to balance the scales of justice, I'm extending a patience I wouldn't normally extend here."

"I appreciate that. These people are with one of the mafias. Yes, that's what I'm saying."

"What the hell are you talking about?"

"There's the Irish Mafia in the church and police. The Jewish Mafia in psycho-analysis, Hollywood, and the literature of the '50s. There's the Indian Mafia on Sixth Street restaurant row as well as the subway newsstands. The Korean green-grocer Mafia. The Gay Mafia of the beat generation. Not to mention the Black Mafia in Harlem, the Russian Mafia in Brighton Beach, the Armenian Carpet Mafia…"

"Enough!" he put his hand up. "Son, you need help…" He rambled on. I had lost him, and saw that a supreme authority was required, the emergency cord, the goiter, an all-unifying force in a fragmented world. A rainbow organ, a multicultural growth, a great democracy of cells. I seized the goiter in both hands like a fallen sparrow and whispered sweet caresses into it. He shrieked, and the yuppies charged me. Court officers dashed in and helped them press the right side of my face to the marble floor. The judge ordered them to take me outside and set me free. The case was dismissed.

I don't know what became of the urine specimen.

Even I know I shouldn't have touched him. I'm convinced that some kind of mind-controlling inhalant was in that soda spilled on me in the cattle-call area. In the past, I had always been afraid of goiters. Once again, they had made a fool of me.

Two weeks later, an unoriginal countersuit arrived in the mail. They and the Japanese, no imagination, the lot of them, just replicating and mass-marketing the ideas invented by the likes of us. I had to appear in court, and it wasn't landlord-tenant court, either.

It was the kind of court that had a bench, but the judge didn't let you approach it. In fact, everyone seemed to shun me, even my Legal Aid lawyer, who seemed to feel that I had somehow gotten him in trouble. Whenever I humbly asked him a question, he'd reply with rolling eyes and opening lines like, "For the millionth time…" or "You again?!" A goiter in that courtroom would have been macheted from the neck like a coconut. I didn't even bother to bring the "wall picture."

In front of the H.U.A.C. hearings in Hollywood, Sterling Hayden had denounced his former mistress. Clifford Odets named J. Edward Bromberg, whom he had just eulogized. Screenplayist Martin Berkley had rattled off 161 names. When Amy got up in the witness box and wagged her finger at me, I knew how the former mistress, the late Mr. Bromberg, and 161 names must have felt. When she started her denunciation, my flimsy, wonton noodle-like heart started flapping like an angel fish on a table top. I had loved (realized an adversarial polarity for) her.

They had all those macho, archetype-possessed men testify against me. They had the cops testify against me. They had the workmen testify against me (they commented on the smallness of my reagan). They had my former co-workers at the Strand Bookstore testify against me. They dredged up an old school teacher to testify against me. They established beyond all reasonable doubt that I was a failure. Initially, I was just an under-achiever and undisciplined, but gradually they slipped in words like recalcitrant and incorrigible. They read from a print-out of my T.R.W. credit history. It indicated that I had defaulted on my student loan. I didn't have a bank account and I was unable to get credit cards. In short, I was a bad risk, kept gaspingly alive in this dusking age of undeserved entitlements.

Then they went through great pains to vindicate society. America was strong. I was its runt. Opportunities were plentiful. Incentives were ubiquitous. The courtroom was pure, I was its speck. We might have won in Vietnam if guys like me hadn't protested and then moved to Canada. The prosecutor put forward some far-fetched theory that I had been sent by the Japanese to oversee the fall of America. He gave an outlandish image reminiscent of the rooftops in Saigon loaded with refugees vying with each other to board evacuating helicopters.

My lawyer didn't object; he was too busy flossing his teeth with an embossed business card. Even if he did object, the judge probably would have overruled him. The general thesis was that I had come from the right side of the tracks and had gone to the wrong side. I had only myself to blame. I was once lean, quick, and handsome. They proved how through self-will I had turned short, fat, and dumb. It was as if the promising side of me was suing the lazy side of me.

Also, many of the statements that would bring the inevitable judgment to a speedy appeal were stricken from the record. Other things occurred that simply eluded the record. For instance, I repeatedly caught the judge giving the plaintiff a nod of familiarity, a wink of complicity.

Wolf down wads of cotton candy, blocks of fruitcake in

brandy sauce, a storm of Hostess Snowballs, a toilet bowl full of Lime Jello from a hospital cafeteria, prunes in heavy syrup from a parochial school. Pepper it with headcheese, Scooterpies, kale. Then, as a chaser, add a six-pack of Colt 45 tall-boys and do some high-impact aerobics. You'll feel the bottled-up nausea I had to hold in. And you'll understand why I suddenly bolted to my feet and yelled, "Lies! Fascism! Totalitarianism! Death of Justice!"

"Objection, your honor!" screamed the attorney for the plaintiff.

"You're blowing our case!" screamed my attorney, who was also for the plaintiff.

"Shut up both of you!" said the judge, to my shock and delight. All eyes, like spotlights, were upon me, and for a moment I was in command. I had complete faith that if I could unify that fragmentation of knowledge into the correct blend of words, like the right digits of a combination lock, I could indeed get what I wanted.

"Young man, I will not have accusations like that bandied about in my courtroom. Do you have something pertinent to tell the court?"

"Yes I do, sir."

"Make the oath, take the stand."

The court officer rambled, I said "I do," and did. "Well, it's like this. This is a case of the rich squeezing the artist out of his workplace because they've turned their own homes into beehives of boredom."

"Ah, then you're an artist?"

"Yes sir."

"Well, I'm quite sympathetic to that. Indeed, I work for the Volunteer Lawyers for the Arts," he said. I glanced over to their lawyer and I could see him unbuttoning his top button behind his tight little tie knot. God was on my side this time.

"What paintings have you painted?" he asked.

"I'm a writer," I said.

"Ahhh, prose, playwright, or bard?"

"None, your honor."

"Essays? Journalism?"

"Well, I'm pursuing histories."

"Well, what histories have you written?" he asked impatiently.

"None, really. I'm planning on bringing history to the masses."

"How?"

"Well, let's be honest, Your Honor, sitcoms are the popular venue."

"So what you're saying is you write screenplays?"

"Not quite," I replied, "I'm on the idea-pitching level of the writing pyramid. I can hire some grad student to put the idea into words."

"Pitching?"

"Well, I mean, I'm working on a cinematic treatment of world history…"

"Cinematic treatment. In my day, we used to call that a novel."

"Your honor, let's be honest, the written word is dead."

"I see," he grinned a bit. "So you're one of those people that always introduce themselves as writers, but quietly believe the written word is dead."

"Yes sir."

"You're a bad name to those few, poor, struggling writers who genuinely scratch, scramble, sacrifice, and do write!"

"I…"

"You'll sit back in your seat and not another word from you, idea-pitcher!" I quietly returned to my seat, and the attorney for the plaintiff spent the remainder of the day insulting me, then I went home.

On the last day of the inquisition, I realized that the judge, with his large jaw, thin lips, and wire-framed glasses, looked vaguely liked Vyshinsky, Stalin's chief prosecutor during the purges. I anticipated the sentence. He'd point at me: "Take Mister Vowels here, the 'pitcher,' to a garage filled with old trucks, turn on the engines to drown out the gunshots, and away with him!"

Well, that wasn't quite it. I was to stay something like ten kilometers away from the plaintiff and stop harassing her. If I persisted in harassing her, I would be sent to Riker's Island. He said, "You would be subject to the pangs of an overcrowded prison." Pangs rhymed with gangs, and overcrowding implied there'd be a tight fit—gang-raped, macho-male-homo-inmate style was the explicit implication. In the words of inner-city youth James Ramseur, victim/villain in the "subway vigilante" Bernie Goetz case—the municipal trial of its day—replying to the cross-examinations of Goetz defense attorney Barry Slotnick, "I know what time it is!"

Walking home through lower New York, I felt depressed. To paraphrase E.B. White, I was seventy-something blocks from where preppie-victim Jennifer Dawn Levin had been strangled, thirty blocks from where graffiti-artist Michael Stewart had been killed, sixty blocks from where homeless Joyce Brown was snatched from the gutter and "rehabilitated," a hundred and thirty-odd blocks from where Eleanor Bumpurs had been bumped off with "necessary force," a state away from New Jersey, and I was slowly heading in the direction of where both John Lennon and Malcolm X had been blasted away.

CHAPTER EIGHT
QUIT YER LOOKIN' AT ME

Unlike TV, fate had let evil once again rule out over good. But fate never let things get too evil, otherwise things would destroy themselves, and there'd be no more evil or TV. When I arrived home, I felt depressed and lonely. I turned on the TV. It advertised one of those party-line numbers "where you can hold a party on the phone." I dialed. For two minutes while I seethed, eight unidentifiable people with the same voice said hello over and over.

She was a growing evil, a cistern collecting power. She had sucked the life forces out of me. I was estranged from my self-esteem and securities. I could kill her and then myself. It was a fair trade; she was as evil as I was good. Besides, the mild sentences dispensed by our criminals' justice system made crime quite appealing; hell, I could probably get out of prison while I was still relatively young. I had far more faith in the criminals' justice system as a criminal than I did as a victim.

How should I do it? I started drinking coffee and doing some drugs to help me think more clearly. The possibilities were endless, and as the drugs catapulted me to greater heights, and my anger became more rampant, each new idea—like rungs of a sadistic ladder—lifted me higher than the prior thought. I worked my way up to abducting her, drugging her, then shackling her, keeping her conscious. If she came down with the flu, I'd fussingly nurse her back to health before continuing the torture. When I'd squeezed out the ultimate drop of pain from her eviscerated body, and she'd finally died, I'd either disappear to Alaska and live with all those burnt-out Vietnam vets or vanish in Arizona with all the pedophile priests.

My fantasy was interrupted by a knock at the door, and there she stood—my tormentor, my future victim, alone, ready.

"May I speak to you a minute?"

I will be your destroyer and therefore I am your maker, I thought in my drugged-out state, but I only said, "What?"

"About today, about this whole thing."

"I want you out of my house," I said, instead of saying, *I will eat your innards.*

"This half of the house is mine." She pointed to the front half of my apartment. "I just was hoping that maybe we could be on some kind of cordial basis, since we're neighbors."

"I'm afraid not. I hate you more than anybody ever hated anyone else throughout both recorded and unrecorded history as well as future history and, for that matter, transcending all planes of possible consciousness throughout our bowl-shaped universe as well as all spatial and temporal planes." I had finally loosely said what I really thought.

"Well, I don't really believe that. Do you want me to tell you what I think?"

"Not really."

"I know that I liked you and I think that you liked me, and you had extra room, and I needed the space, and I think that you realized that if we were roommates, maybe we could become closer."

"What do you mean 'closer?'"

She stepped closer. "I mean lovers."

"Lovers?!!" So ironic! Indeed, I had become her devoted, loyal, and eternal hater.

"Ever since I saw you, do you know what I saw?"

"What?"

"A gnarled acorn."

"Flattery won't work."

"An acorn, a seed that if well managed could one day sprout and become a magnificent oak."

"Oh?"

"Do you know what I sometimes see myself as?"

"What?"

"Rich, fertile soil."

"Really?"

"I can help you."

"How?"

"You're unemployed. You're unwashed. You're eating the wrong foods, reading the wrong books, rutted in very bad habits."

"That's what I am."

"Suppose I told you that you could have consonants in your name instead of all those subversive vowels."

"Consonants?"

"Suppose I told you that you could be tall."

"Tall? What do I have to do?"

"Just trust me."

"You're wicked. You're trying to take what remains of my apartment and sanity away."

"Suppose I tore up the lease. Suppose I signed a statement saying that my stay here was subject to your day-to-day approval."

"Wha?"

"Suppose I tore down the wall?"

"Cha?"

"Suppose I tore off my work clothes and lived with you as a supportive wife. Suppose I propped you up when you were weak and praised you when you were strong?"

"Xzk?"

"Suppose you disposed of all those profane old magazines,

and I became your love-slave, your centerfold, your sperm bank."

"[@#|?"

I sputtered and spurted in my pants. I felt my heart bulging as if a charred sausage link were stuck sideways in my esophagus. It was immediately apparent that all hatred was just sexual polarity for her. Everything started tightening as I said, "I la...I laav..."

"What?!"

"I love ya." A tight fist that wouldn't unclasp was in my chest; I couldn't breathe. "I'm having a heart attack!" I gasped as I dropped to the floor. I had always intended to have CPR instructions tattooed on my chest, but, like everything else, I'd never got around to it. I saw a long dark tunnel. I was speeding through it. It was kind of a superb subway ride free of beggars, turnstile jumpers, and rats. I wasn't scared. I knew I was dead, and then a pinpoint of light appeared in the way-off: God. I asked him if psycho-comedian Andy Kaufman was really dead, or just perpetrating his greatest, driest gag.

As if I was a non-refundable beer can, he simply said, "Returneth."

I felt shifted in reverse, going backward, and then from up on the ceiling, I could see Amy pounding on my chest. Responsibly, she had attended the Red Cross classes. While she was mouth-to-mouthing me, I tried tongue-kissing her. Instead, I gagged and passed out.

I awoke in a hospital with tubes in my arm and mouth and nose, and beeping from the electrocardiogram in my ear. My entire corpus appeared wound up in toilet paper; my legs had casts. My face was bandaged and it felt swollen. I also felt a numb weight on my chest. Between the slits of gauze, I slowly started inspecting my surroundings. I saw a figure slumped over in a seat in the far side of the room—her.

"You," I groaned inaudibly, and made a pathetic attempt at finding that umbilical nurse-button. Despite the fact that I was incredibly weak—it felt as if they had peeled the muscles from my bones—I was terrified. I was sure that she had tried to kill me. Here she was again to finish the job. She could simply grab the pillow out from under my head and put it over my face. After a desperate struggle for the little button, I fell exhausted back to sleep.

I woke up an indeterminate amount of time later. She was still there. Was she patiently waiting for my demise? That deluded dream about her wanting to be my sperm bank, what crapola. No doubt she had observed that my diet consisted largely of greasy fast foods, and she must have realized that along with my poor habits, a screeching halt in that old yellow cab of my ill-maintained body could send everything tumbling forward. But what was she doing here? Even more, why had she let me live this long?

"Will he be okay?" she asked the nurse who was checking a series of needles, tubes, bottles, and beeping electrical graphs as if she were adjusting the transmission of a compact car.

"He'll be just fine," the lady in white replied, and left. Amy looked down at me. She kissed and massaged my cold hand and started crying and saying things into my limp metacarpal. I must have had a partial stroke because it was still remarkably difficult to talk.

"Why are you treating me this way?" I said slowly.

"You're awake!" she exclaimed, hugging me.

"Huh?"

"I love you," she said without mitigation or hesitance. "I always fight when put on the defensive, and you have this way of putting a girl very much on the defensive. But I also realized that in many ways you're everything that I was ever looking for. When I wasn't with you, I realized that I couldn't stop thinking about you. Have you ever felt that way?"

Yes, I had a severe rash once. When I wasn't scratching, I was thinking about scratching it. I managed to bend my mouth, a smile. Yes, I loved (adversarial polarity) and wanted her, but I still couldn't understand her infatuation for me.

Slowly, I ground out words: "Can't you find anyone else? Is your life really this lonely?"

"Of course not," she replied, "Whitlock wants wedlock. He's mad about me."

"Where did you meet him?"

"Society affairs."

"Why are you picking me?" I replied slowly.

"Well, in a word, for me it's always been a case of likes repelling."

"And opposites attracting?" I wheezed out.

"Not entirely. I've always been very sensitive around invalids and sickly types. They disturb me. I can't stay with an irregular person; people who are handicapped or freakish make me sick to my stomach. Quite bluntly, I'm a complete Darwinist. I think runts like yourself should be drowned like kittens. I'm completely opposed to medical technology's bent for preserving aberrations that never should be permitted. But the truth is, the closest I can really come to love is pity. In fact, I'm completely embarrassed about my love for you. Indeed, you're more of a perversion to me, and perversions are stronger than conventional loves because they're predicated on one's greatest fears and weaknesses. I really wish I could get out from under these feelings for you. They must be kept in utter secrecy."

I asked her why I had all these additional bandages on my body and casts on my arms and legs.

"Well, that's why I can confess my love for you now."

"Huh?"

"I had to do some alterations."

"What?"

"There are some things you should know."

"What?"

"When they brought you in, you desperately needed a bypass."

"And I'm sure it won't be my last. So what?"

"They searched for your relatives, but we couldn't find any. Do you have parents?"

"I didn't break out of a shell!" I replied laboriously, not admitting I was adopted, which might have led to the possibility that I was hatched.

"Well, we couldn't locate anyone, so I said I was your wife, and with the assistance of a couple of doctors who were fairly mercenary, and since I love you, and…" She paused.

"What is it?!" I murmured a shout.

"I took the liberty of having some elective surgery done on you."

"Elective? What was done?"

"Now, I'll pay for everything. You really don't have to worry about that, you're an investment."

"A what?"

"Like the apartment, I had you completed before I moved in."

"What?"

"You had a total of seven," she explained, "not counting the rhinoplasty and the liposuction. You've had nine operations. And you're scheduled for one more."

"Nine operations! What the fuck…"

"Oh, no, I elected against that one. I didn't think you needed a penis augmentation."

"What!" I started squirming against a network of bandages and restrainers. What kind of Michael Jackson had she turned me into?

"You shouldn't struggle," she said. "The operation done on your legs is highly experimental. They've never tried it on mammals before. You could rip the arteries."

"My legs? What was done to my legs?!"

"They call it 'bone accentuation.' A part of the torso-proportioning."

"Huh?"

"You're average height now."

"What? What's this?"

"And thin, too."

"What? Where's my fat!"

"You've had radical fat suction."

"Out!"

"You still have a pupil-fusion operation tomorrow."

"What?"

"Brilliant blue eyes that actually glow in the dark, like little blue headlights."

"Get the hell out of here! I swear I'll have you arrested. I'll see you behind bars."

"All right, calm down." She rose to go. "You're tall, thin, and handsome. Get used to it, Bane."

"Bane? Who the hell's Bane?" Yet the name rang a bell.

"I decided that you'd make a good Bane. I plan to call you Bane during the length of our relationship."

"Get the fuck OUT!" I hollered and screamed until I was so frantic that the sound frequency of the electro-cardiograph blended into one long single beep. To my continued screams, Amy calmly left.

When an orderly entered, I screamed obscenities until he called a nurse. I kept screaming until a doctor rushed in. From him I asked exactly what had been done to me and was told of one big life-saving operation and a variety of smaller forays into my body.

He itemized it for me: My face was different. The eyes were almondine, the nose, retrouseè, the cheekbones were reinforced. The chin was clefted, the jawbone strengthened. My ear lobes were connected to my jaw. In short, I was handsome. The balding field of my scalp was seeded with a new crop of hair, the skin sanded. He went on. I informed the good doctor that unless I was prepped stat! for operations reversing the dubious damage, his hospital would collapse under the weight of my Chungking lawsuit. He informed me that this was quite impossible for a variety of reasons. Not the least of which was the fact that experts had been called from all corners of the U.S. Millions of dollars in operations and procedures had changed hands over my body. Articles delineating the many surgeries were currently in galley form and about to be printed. Amy had gone even further than the mass operations done in Bismarck, North Dakota. She had made me supremely into one of her own.

Over the next few weeks, while recuperating from the surgery, when I wasn't unsuccessfully hunting for big-name trial lawyers who would competently handle my case, I spent the hours flipping through an odd assortment of fragranced, glossy magazines, either men's fashion magazines, mainly *GQ*, or business magazines, like *Forbes*. Gaze on anything long enough and you'll learn to love it. I gradually developed a fixation on shady, showy figures of film, fashion, and finance.

I found myself watching that air-time-purchased TV show, *The Millionaire Makers*, desperately trying to follow the "no-money-down process" to becoming a financial wizard. Venture capitalism was on my mind. As a pastime, on little scraps of paper, I began fooling with unusual plans and byzantine schemes: If I could sell the lease of my apartment for such and such, and get a second mortgage, and invest that capital in such and such, before this so-and-so takeover, and then liquidate the assets into X bonds, I'd be worth X zillions in just a few years.

CHAPTER NINE
VENGEANCE IS MINE
(KARMA IS FOR PUSSIES)

As the bandages were peeled off, the results were quite embarrassing. It all eluded me at first, but in the mirror of popular opinion, I beheld it. As the gauzy veils unspooled, a sigh went up, like a puff of smoke. I watched with the same goggle-eyed disbelief as the middle-aged nurses who filled the spectator pews in the surgical theater.

"You know, you're lucky," one R.N. remarked, in a nasal, outer-borough honk. "Some folks wait years before their bodies can deteriorate enough for the operations you've had."

How fortunate I was. After all the bandages were off, and I started realizing what I was going to look like and what the future would hold, I felt lightheaded. Good looks were a wild card I had not been dealt. Only in the most incidental way had I even thought of my appearance.

Yet, as the nights progressed, I began to love sleeping with myself. During the days, intensive therapy was the regimen: hydrotherapy, parallel bars, Nautilus machines—all awakening stringy gristle that never knew it was muscle, spaghetti-tied around newly fused bones. On a daily basis for months, the hours were filled with intensive aerobic and weightlifting sessions. My feelings for me were intensifying. Initially I had just a crush, a puppy love, but eventually I developed an Adele H. obsession with myself.

One day I was awakened by an ominous numb sensation. I opened my eyes to see the ghastly Whitlock standing before me, pinching an I.V. tube that had been dripping Lord-knows-what into my gorgeous arm.

"Hi, handsome, remember me?" he dropped the tube and began. "We've got a problem to work out."

"Leave me very much alone," I pleaded.

"Very much like to. Very much like to. But you seem to constantly be stuck in my craw."

"What do you want?"

"Amy seems to think you're a god in rags."

"I'll sue the bitch if I ever see her again, I swear. Look what she did to me." I was still hypocritically irate over her five-hour body makeover.

"You don't look any different to me. But I'm glad to see you feel this way."

"I'll sue you, too, I swear."

"Suppose we settle this right now."

"How?"

"Suppose I give you a solid figure, and we put an end to all this squabbling."

"What kind of figure?"

"Suppose I give you, say, ten thousand bucks, and in exchange, you just stay away from us."

"You mean give up my apartment?"

"Yeah."

"No way."

"How about fifty thousand, cold hard cash up front. That's a lot of money."

"You think I'm some hick?"

"You stay away from me and Amy, and I'll deposit a hundred thousand bucks into your personal account."

"I don't have an account."

"All right, I'll give it to you, but I want a year."

"Just keep her away from me," I countered.

"Fuck you," he said as if it were a salutation.

"Fuck you, too," I saluted him back, and he left.

During that entire duration, while the hospital kept getting Amy's checks, subsidizing my journey into ever-unfolding beauty, she didn't reappear once. They soon moved me to a place outside the city that was more of a sanctuary. Weeks turned to months, and months gave way to seasons. I reasoned that she saw this as payment for stealing my apartment, and I assumed that under Whitless's ocean of wealth she was able to extinguish any alleged love for me.

When most of the physical therapy was complete, I was informed that I'd be allowed to live at home and come in to the hospital for daily workouts and checkups.

Inasmuch as each of us is the center of our own universe, it takes no effort to believe that we are gods and should be treated accordingly. During the time in the hospital, when all the money and attention was being spent on me, I wasn't compelled in the slightest to wonder why. I was me and therefore worth all the money in the world. To me, bad as they were, my farts always came out smelling like roses.

Good fortune has a way of making even the most bitter mind magnanimous. This *jihad* with Amy had gone on long enough. I was soon well enough to check out. Hopefully she and asshole would have moved off somewhere and killed each other with their selfish and surgical forms of love.

On my first day home, I walked across the hallway and knocked on her door. I wanted to set the matter straight. Getting no response, I went to my adjacent door. At the base of it, I found a sealed envelope. Tearing it open, I found a VISA card made out in the name Joseph Aeiou. Inside was a letter:

Aeiou,

Here's a company credit card with the first install-ment, five thousand dollars of credit. In return, all I ask

*is that you leave me and the mother of my future chil-
dren alone, and you will receive more money with time.
This is my last effort at being nice. If this continues I'll
have to be…not so nice.*

*Andrew Whitlock,
M.B.A. Harvard, 1958*

I slipped the note into my pocket and entered my
home. Aggg! My apartment was a wreck. A typhoon had
passed through it. The furniture was destroyed. My clothing
and belongings were piled around the place. Filth, debris,
profanity everywhere.

In short, it was exactly as I had left it. After two months of
living like a king in a hospital, I had cultivated both a need
and an admiration for purpose and structure.

I stepped into the waking nightmare, dreading the pri-
mordial things growing chaotically around the refrigerator
and sink. I feared the hostile communities of insects and
rodents with which I had clumsily coexisted in the past. They
had bloomed and multiplied. Two sabre-toothed mice with
thick, woolly coats held their ground and stared indignantly
when I entered their living room. 'You dash and dive into
some filthy crack,' they seemed to say.

Flying waterbugs and other bespeckled lotus-like insects
swarmed on the neglected Fritos, uneaten Hostess products,
melted ice cream, and funky onion dip which I had eaten for
dinner and left on the counter just before the heart attack.

Upon inspecting the burlap texture and urine odor of my
old clothing, which I had once so thoughtlessly pressed
against my now silky skin, I was retroactively sickened. If I
needed an added reason for a new wardrobe, all my prior garments were of irregular dimensions for a squat fatty.

After a couple hours of shopping at Macy's way above my
plastic power, I handed the cashier girl my card and chewed
my bottom lip to see whether its magic would take. She asked

for ID, I pulled out my old college ID, and she made doubtful expressions, while trying to compare me with the fiend in the photo.

Desperately, I stuck my fingers in my nose making it more bulbous. I pulled back my hairline to give her a taste of my former baldness. I squashed my cheeks together to indicate my poor skin, loose jowls, and multiple chins.

Finally, nervously, she returned the plastic wand with a receipt. I went off to the Herald Center. With bags and boxes containing all the styles and fashions that I had once mocked in glossy magazines, I was ready to leave. But first, exhausted by my little shopping safari, and hoping to delay returning to the hellhole apartment, I dropped into a midtown trap for a watery, tourist-bilking beer.

Usually, I would order a pitcher and work my way to the dregs. But here I was with this nice, new body and I had already ground one carcass into hamburger meat. So I just ordered a single headless, lite beer and sipped it very slowly.

Three cute girls who looked *90210*-esque were laughing it up at the other end of the bar. Looking them over, I realized that they were all staring at me and giggling. Since the '70s, I couldn't help comparing tripletted babes to *Charlie's Angels*, but they didn't look anything like *Charlie's Angels*. I kind of shuffled over, approaching the one that looked least like Farrah (Majors (O'Neal)) Fawcett. I said, "Hi."

"Hi," returned the one who looked nothing like Jaclyn Smith.

"What do you kids do?" I asked the one without any resemblance to Kate Jackson.

"We're actresses," replied the non-Farrah-esque.

"Really? I'm kind of a director of intelligent, low-budget, poorly distributed films."

"What kind of films do you do?" asked one or all of them.

"Mainly adaptations of wordy, anglophile novels of the latter part of the last century."

"Why?" they or she asked.

"Because there's a bunch of people who don't read books anymore, but feel real guilty about it, so they figure that by punishing themselves through these tedious films, they're filling their reading quota for the year."

One at a time they responded:

"Don't the actors not get too much money…"

"…Or exposure…"

"…For it?"

"That's true," I said suavely, "but I make them appear far more intelligent than they'll ever really be. And no one has to take off their clothes."

"Wow!" They raced with the bait. Then one of them asked, "Are you from Europe? You seem to have kind of an accent."

"Well," I replied Daniel Day-Lewisly, "I am in something of a self-exile. New York is a natural Elba. Don't you agree?" They all giggled, so I continued, "Few realize that among New York's many former expatriates one must count both Trotsky and Talleyrand."

"How fascinating," they chirped.

Out the bullshit kept rushing. I couldn't believe that all this was happening, and I kept wondering, why are they buying this? But then I remembered I was good-looking, a homonym for right, a synonym for everything profitable. Usually I just didn't get a response. (If lucky, I earned an insult.) But my looks now were a catapult from which I could sling forth endless crap. Eventually, we all went to one of their apartments in Kip's Bay. I unloaded my bags near the door, and we examined the flat. It had a lot of rooms, and we spent the evening giggling, drinking wine coolers, playing Nintendo, and watching MTV. Subtly, I'd sneak off with them one at a time to a different room and slip one hand up the blouse, the other down the pants, past the elastic guards and straps, and feel them up, one at a time, twice as fast. Aside from the dewy warmth and pointy tips, all I could think was—Wow! Even I felt like tipping them off: Can't you see it!? He's a slinky!

It wasn't like I was even horny. I just felt like I had to get away with it. Soon, when two-thirds of them faced the hard fact that I probably wouldn't marry them—which is the only reason most chicks ever let you space out on them—they departed.

I was left alone with non-Farrah. I entered her bedroom, where she was spread out against a vast collection of stiletto-high heels, an Imelda ready for her Ferdinand. After some preliminary handiwork, I realized that I could usurp her, a rebel uprising. All my life I had been starving, with only morsels of memories to sustain me. This chick was undoubtedly the best looking thing I had ever conned into the sack. But suddenly I understood that even though Joseph Aeiou could do no better, I, Bane, could only do better. I was a diamond cutter with a cheap mood ring.

I remember reading how Hugh Hefner, during his middle-aged, pre-AIDS heyday, kept a blue book filled with notes on all the chicks he'd made it on. It was complete with notes on where he put his dapper reagan and everything. If possible, he would even videotape the spectacle. He had boxes full of economy-size Johnson's Baby Oil carried in, sometimes on a weekly basis, by workmen who had to keep from snickering as they marched through the mansion. Presumably, they had to leave the boxes in the bathroom. The non-Farrah's bathroom was adjacent to the front door. Claiming I had to squeeze a dump, I grabbed my Herald Square shopping bags and snuck out.

On the way home, I saw the all-night pharmacy on Fiftieth Street and Lexington Avenue. I quickly picked up some Blistex, Vaseline Intensive Care, and a few other protective medications. I had to take care of my new-and-improved self.

When I got to my building, it was about 3:00 a.m., and I had to return to the same contemptible apartment that that slime Joseph had lived in. Sticking the key in, opening the lock and door, I entered loudly, flicking the lights off and on in hope of scaring away the wildlife. I was greeted by disbelief. It was beautiful, as if my world had been beautified along with me. In the space of twelve hectic hours, most of the garbage, including boxes and clothes, had disappeared, and a connecting door had been quickly constructed into the adjoining Berlin wall between Amy and me. I threw my boxes of new clothes on a couch and called for Amy. She wasn't there. Nervously, I tried her door. It was unlocked. I went into her new bathroom. Whole walls were covered with magnification mirrors and bright bulbs. I opened some of the dermatological products I had purchased.

I started putting on applicants and creams, I don't know why. I had never done it before. I spent hours doing the inexplicable. Time that I would normally invest in either intellectual acquisition or piggish habits was, instead, devoted to skin care. Soon there was a knock at her door. I had no idea who it was.

"Go away." I didn't want to do anything but work on myself. But the door opened anyway. It was Amy. From out in the hallway, I heard Whitlock appealing, "But look at the xeroxed letter and this credit card printout. He's sold you out for the price of a wardrobe."

"Then I respect him that much more."

"I love you," Whitlock invoked.

"I'm only interested in you professionally!" she replied. "Now leave me alone, old man!"

I had a magnifying glass and was carefully searching for irregularity in skin texture, only noticing her peripherally. She was dressed in some "sexy" Frederick's of Hollywood lace. Suddenly I had a rush of excitement: A just-visible dot, which I suspect was a speck from a cigarette ash, was lodged deep in one of my forehead pores. Carefully, I extracted the speck, a pimple aborted. For the first time I had an idea of the thrill that pulsates through a pimple-popper.

"I'm glad to see you've finally taken an interest in yourself," I heard her say. She was leaning against the bathroom door. I looked over at her. For the first time, she seemed extraordinarily plain. She kept talking about how much she had cared for me and how all spats that we had in the past were just an indication of this care. She slowly approached me. I think it was an attempt at being romantic. When she came between me and my mirror, I stepped even closer to her, attempting to see my reflection in her eyes.

"Bottom line," she said, "I love you."

"I love you, too," I said to myself reflected in her eyes.

"Oh, Bane!"

"I worship you, I…I…" I couldn't believe how strikingly handsome I was. I was hypnotized by my own eyes. Yet, I had to admit it, the brilliant, blue pupils that glowed in the dark were my one sin of omission. Still, I had to see more of me in different lights. I picked up a hand mirror and danced around with it. I was energized by seeing myself. I was something that transcended sexes. Hermaphroditically handsome. I was my own lock-and-key, I felt sure I could self-produce, I could cleave like a hydra upon orgasm.

I was above standard morality. I could do more, understand more, jump higher than an ugly or plain person could. I couldn't understand how come I wasn't followed, pursued, exalted, lionized, and worshipped. Adulation and prostrations were lavished on things of far less beauty. I went over to the window and looked down at the moving gray mass, like squirming brain tissue—meaningless commuters.

In some great overwhelming and predestined surge, I raced out the door, down the flutter of steps, and onto the streets filled with the morning rush hour. In my right hand I still clenched my scepter of power, the hand mirror.

Jumping onto the hood of a parked car, I stared into the mirror and screamed to multi-legged men-o-pede: "Run to your false prophets, inspect the photos and trinkets on your altars, and compare. Notice the sentimental Bambi-eyes of Christ! See the ragged turban on Mohammed! The large, oily forehead of Lenin and booger-like mole on Madonna's upper lip! Observe disproportions, imperfections, and flaws of both a structural and aesthetic nature. If you saw them on the street, would they be living embodiments of their truths? Would you instantly recognize and be faithful? Behold me! My beauty has been laid bare. My deep and undeniable philosophy exudes through me—an onomatopoeia of truth. Hidden and intensive meaning has been exhumed from me. I give this era and place definition high above other periods and places. You live in the age of Bane!"

I hugged myself. I kissed myself passionately on the lips. I tried sticking my tongue down my throat. An erection knifed upward and still more blood filled; my reagan was in extreme pain. I groped at me in lewd, yet sincere ways. I dropped down to my knees. My head was spinning, arrhythmic pulses; suddenly I vomited...

Quickly, Amy, still in lingerie, hustled through the maddening crowd, pulled the mirror out of my hand, and shoved a paper bag over my head. In a moment I passed out.

Sometime later I awoke back in the apartment, the bag still on my head. I could hear a male voice whispering, "We had a deal, Aeiou!"

"Shut up or leave!" Amy shrieked. It was the Shadow—Whitlock.

"Look," I heard, "here's the company credit card I gave him to leave you. And look at these receipts! His use of the card is proof of his willingness to dump you!"

"SHUT UP!" Amy yelled, "Are you okay, Bane?"

"I think I had some kind of...ego avalanche," I explained through a mouth hole I poked out of the bag with my tongue.

"Vanity," Whitlock decrepitly replied, "he's become vain about his looks."

"Are you okay?" she asked.

"I guess I have to find something new that's ugly about me. New ruffles..."

"Shouldn't be too hard," I heard Whitlock mutter.

"All this is very difficult. My thoughts have been taking on a new and sensible turn. I've been thinking in short, declarative sentences. And worse, I…I…"

"Do you hear that, Whitlock?" Amy said to the monster.

"Elaborate," replied Whitlock.

"I've secretly been considering a ca…ca…" The word was obscene, the phrase had turned men into machines. I dreaded saying it, but there it was, "Career!"

"What?"

"I've been making plans!"

"Plans!?"

"For the last couple of weeks, I've been thinking about making myself more efficient and goal-ridden within the common value-systems."

"What value-systems?"

"Money-making, power consolidation, social acceptance. I mean, never before have I cared about what other people thought of me. Now I'm filled with doubts and wonder, like maybe all my learning is just gratuitous. If knowledge can't be utilized or, more important, be instrumental in reaching a precise financial return, it's unjustified."

"Do you hear him, Whitlock? It's over." I could imagine her silly, syllogistic thinking process at work: Money was meaning, ergo I was meaningful.

"Give him time," Whitlock rushed in, "He has no staying power. In no time at all he'll backslide into the same slothful sybarite."

"Test him!" Amy replied.

"Test me for what?"

"Exactly," Whitlock replied. "Test him for what? He has the same desires as the rest of us."

"What are your desires?" I asked Amy, wondering if we were truly of one mind.

"Amy wants to be a self-made millionaire," Whitlock spoke up.

"And once you're a millionaire?" I asked. "What then?"

"I want to travel," she uttered modestly behind an embarrassed smile.

"To be a dekillionaire!" Whitlock corrected her in a sky-shaking boom. "Amy then strives to be a dekillionaire."

"And then?" I asked Whitlock, who appeared to be acting as her truthful side.

"To be a hektillionaire," Whitlock asserted.

"Wait a second," I heard her mutter.

"How can you treat yourself so well?" the liberal jerk in me needed to know. "How can you want so much while others, just as human as you, are starving?"

"Maybe," Whitlock joined in, "just maybe all people are not equal. And maybe, just because people like us do succeed, it doesn't mean we rob you of success. Maybe people like you fail on your own." It was like listening to Scrooge teach the Spirit of Christmas the error of his kindly ways.

"Get the hell out of here!!" Amy finally belted out. "Get out! You're repulsive."

As I saw her shove the most eligible bachelor since [the late] John John [before he married, and accidentally killed, Carolyn Bessette] right out the door and slam it, I felt that deep sense of gratitude that was frequently and falsely advertised as love.

I went over to her and held her tight, and sincerely explained, "I'd be honored to be your roommate, but I just don't know if I can. I just don't think it would be a realistic match."

"I hardly think your criterion of reality is anything to judge anything by," she replied curtly.

"What is that supposed to mean?"

"You've bungled one thing after another. Andrew told me how you met, how you initially scared the hell out of him. He didn't just pick on you out of the blue."

"Did he tell you how he cut my grant money?"

"He doesn't owe you an education. He only started the endowment in honor of a relative who died in his arms."

"Who was this?"

"I don't know, he doesn't talk about it. All I know is it happened in Tokyo in the early '60s. He wouldn't mention it. I suspect it might have been a son."

"A son? Well, that doesn't excuse other things he did."

"What other things?" she asked.

"Did he tell you how he humiliated me on a stage at *YUK!* and screwed my girlfriend?"

"There's another example of your gripless reality. He claims that she was not your girlfriend, he didn't screw her, and that you were a hit at the comedy club." Everything I said was a barefaced lie; every opinion was fundamentally wrong. Another comfirmation that I had met my true match. Adversarial polarity was achieved.

I had no choice but to be with this woman. She was the only one I had ever met that would not allow me to lie to myself. The only person that could truly hurt me. Furthermore, she was the only person who would demand nothing short of excellence from me—not that she'd get it. And besides, I desperately wanted to screw her.

"All right, fine," I said. "How shall we do this? We already live together so shall we make my room the living room and your house the bedroom, or vice versa?"

"What do you mean? Who said anything about a restructuring?"

"I thought we loved each other." I didn't dare launch into the adversarial polarity philosophy. Women can't bear dark, stark realism. After a lifetime of being babied and wooed, they like soft lighting, sweet-smelling, sugary-tasting, laughter-inducing stuff, and who could blame them?

"Even if we did love each other," she replied, "that doesn't imply that we should become inseparably connected until we merge into a single bland person."

"Did you want to have a relationship or what?"

"Bane, I care for you deeply. I find you intriguing, deeply intriguing, and we can try a limited partnership, but first, your eye color scares me. Secondly, I'm late for an appointment now, and, indeed, will probably be late for my next three appointments. But lastly, I can't respect anyone, Bane, who doesn't have a decent livelihood."

"You're absolutely right." She was right.

"I'll call you later," she said, and off she went.

With that she dressed into her office uniform and dashed out the door. It was 10:00 a.m., time for bed.

I went to sleep with the faith that—in the words of the greatly misunderstood and unfairly neglected Captain & Toenail—Love (or adversarial polarity) would keep us together.

I was asleep. The phone started ringing, I awoke and answered it. A frantic voice said, "So what livelihood have you chosen?"

"Who is this?" I replied, still high on sleepitude.

"Me—Amy. What have you done in the space of five hours since I last saw you?"

"Oh, it's you dear. I'm sorry, I was dozing."

"Dozing?! These are the business hours! The wheels are turning! The doers are doing!"

"Yes, but I was up for twelve hours yesterday."

"Twelve hours, ha! This is my thirtieth hour, and I'm fit as a fiddle. You've got to learn to lengthen your biological day."

"My biological day?"

"You can't be a slave to your metabolism. Got to run." Click, she hung up. She probably was actually running. I did love her. She was living a life for the both of us. I felt sure that my life would now work out okay. She watched out for me in the waking world, while I looked out for her in the sleeping world. Slipping…sliding…sleeping…

Ri!i!i!i!i!ng!!! Phone again, I answered and put phone to ear.

"What have you done now?"

"I was looking for work."

"Good. What are we having for dinner tonight?"

"I got some Lays potato chips and onion dip," I said, still drunk on z-z-z's.

"WHAT! Are you insane?"

"No ma'am."

"You have a very serious heart condition. Didn't the doctor give you a lecture on what foods to eat, and exercises???"

"Yes, I wasn't thinking."

"Clearly. I got to go."

"I love…" She hung up.

I went back to sleep.

SLEEP; R!I!N!G! The heart doc was calling at the request of Miss Rapapport to remind me what nutrients I needed and sample dinners that I could ingest. I thanked him, unplugged the phone, and went back to sleep. When I finally awoke it was dark, early evening. But for me it was morning.

The first bad habit that day started with the breakfast of two oily eggs, greasy potatoes, and a beer. Afterwards, I went to the East Village and looked at photo art books with dirty pictures at the center table in the St. Mark's Bookstore. There I bumped into another friend, Cecil, who was going to some vaudevillian transvestite show at a new place that was once the site of the old dance joint called The World, over on Avenue C. I went with him, lost him, got drunk, and fell asleep in one of the big ballroom's bathrooms. When I awoke it was about 6:00. Some strange man in a car stared at me as I stumbled to Houston Street for transportation. When I walked toward him, he zoomed off.

Before hailing a cab, I realized that someone must've gone through my pockets 'cause I had no money. When I got home it was 7:30 a.m. The telephone was ringing. I picked it up. It was my new girlfriend, Amy.

"Where were you?"

"I went out," I said. "Where are you?"

"I came home, got six hours of sleep, and came back to work."

"But you were at work yesterday," I said.

"I put in a seventeen-hour work day. I'm trying to bring it up to twenty."

"But…"

"I don't think we're connecting," she added.

"We're not," I assured her, and then asked, "How much money are you worth?"

"That changes day to day with Mr. Dow Jones. In the neighborhood of two hundred and fifty thousand in stocks and bonds. Why?"

"How could you afford all the operations done on me?"

"I have a great insurance plan. I have you down as a spouse."

"With a quarter-million you can quit and we can live off that for ten to fifteen years."

"Right, and then you're in your forties, without a livelihood. What then?"

"Well, I don't know if you saw that film narrated by Welles."

"Orson Welles?"

"Yeah, he did a film about Nostradamus, who says that New York is going to be blown up soon. We'll all be dead in a few years."

"Let me get this straight," she said, "I'm supposed to plan my life around the predictions of some mystic of the last century."

"Sixteenth century. He mentioned Franco by name."

"Who?"

"Franco, the former dictator of Spain. And he predicted Hitler's rise to power, only he called him Hisler."

"Suppose Nostradamus is wrong. We'll be homeless soon."

"We could always go on welfare."

"Now you listen up," she said. "If you want to remain in this relationship, you're going to have to find a career."

"Huh?"

"I am looking for a professional partner. Do you understand?" She elaborated, "I am looking for someone who I can lunch with in executive dining rooms. Someone to go on junkets and conventions with. You don't have to be managerial, but I at least expect someone gainfully employed."

"But life should be a vacation," I replied. She hung up on me. I laid down and thought awhile. Could she be right? What if Nostradamus was wrong? What if peace in the world were sustained? What if I turned forty and drove another body into the ground? I did need a new course, a way of getting more mileage. To that foggy resolve, I fell asleep. But it didn't last very long.

I awoke to a glass of cold water being thrown on me.

"Up and at'em!" she yelled as I bolted up. "Now! Before you do irreversible damage to your life! Are you or are you not ready to batten down and find an occupation so you won't someday be a bag person?"

"Bu..." Moments earlier I had been in a deep, important sleep.

"What do you want to be?" she asked.

"I don't know—a fireman?" Her stare became so sharp and intense I thought her eyes were going to cross. It was quickly apparent that she wouldn't tolerate that answer.

"I...I...I'm good with my hands," I replied, holding them up for examination.

"Good! Now that's a start." Leaning forward she looked fiercely into the unwashed windows of my bloodshot eyes, as if to read my thoughts more closely than I could.

"Since your operation, you look...rugged," she remarked. "I don't know why, but I see you in overalls."

I released each syllable of the word slowly, "Pro-le-tar-i-an." I remembered a postcard sent to me years ago. The subject of the card was the giant statue of the Futurist poet Mayakovsky in overalls on a pedestal in downtown Moscow. For me, this was the symbol of heroic modern man.

"I'll do anything to wear overalls!" I said heartfully, picturing myself in dungarees with blue straps over my shoulders.

"Great, I have it all mapped out. Dress!" I dressed.

"Come on!" She grabbed and dragged me down the stairs and into a cab. It was then that I noticed the G-man. I remembered him from the other night parked in front of The World. This morning he was sitting across the street in a parked car. He was conspicuously inconspicuous under a fedora and sunglasses. He turned over the engine of his car and followed our cab.

We ended up at the Apex Technical School. The G-man parked across the street. As we went in I told Amy, "A G-man is across the street."

"Whitlock hired a gumshoe," she said with an eye-rolling expression. "If he wants to throw his money away, so be it."

We entered, and she sat me down. A receptionist asked me to take a very basic test before meeting with any of the guidance counselors. I decided to test the test. I took it and deliberately flunked. They said they'd make an exception in my instance and sent me and Amy in to see the counselor.

"What exactly do you want out of Apex?"

"Well…" Amy cut me off before I could say, "A job in which I could wear overalls."

"Training for a job that would provide a starting wage of something in the ballpark of twenty K—starting figure—but with entrepreneurial potential." The virtues of being a welder, an auto mechanic, and a refrigerator repairman were discussed. Each had merits and demerits. Classes, tuition, placement services, and statistics of employability in different job markets were considered. For the next thirty minutes the interview became a dialogue between Amy and the counselor. I quietly sat as my life was mapped out for me. For the most part, I tried listening to the sounds of their words as a dog might attempt to comprehend a human conversation. Occasionally they would look at me for a response. When Amy shook, I shook no. When she nodded, I nodded yes. A strong relationship required the faith and loyalty of a trained seal. Amy furiously jotted down notes. I noticed that she wrote the counselor a personal check, and I assumed I was enrolled in something.

"Is there anything else you'd like to know?" the guidance counselor asked, before we were to take leave.

"I'd just like to ask two questions," I said. It was the first time I spoke.

"Shoot."

"Are tools included?"

"I'm afraid not."

"They are in the commercial."

"That's just TV."

"Are distressed-denim overalls standard issue?"

Amy sighed.

"Well, you certainly may wear them, but many of our students wear either orange or white overalls."

"Fine." We went outside. The G-man was still out there. Amy tried to hail a cab.

"Why don't we get the G-man to drive us. He's going to follow us anyway." She ignored me and got a cab with bad shocks. As our cab pogoed from pothole to pothole and jockeyed wildly from lane to lane, Amy explained my schedule. I was to attend a class in freon management. I had to purchase a face mask, goggles, a pair of industrial rubber gloves, and a funnel through which the freon would be poured into the apparatus. The first class was tomorrow at noon.

"Wait a second!" I stopped her. "What part of a car requires freon?"

"You idiot! It was decided that you were going to study refrigeration and air-condition repair." She explained that there was far more money and marketability in it. She told me where I could purchase the special funnel, and opening her purse, she loaned me the money to purchase it. Then changing the subject, she talked about my getting that last piece of corrective surgery: my pupil-fusion operation.

"Who devised it, Joseph Mengele?"

While she rambled on about how I could have such beautiful baby blues, I envisioned years from now, in the early part of the twenty-first century, standing in front of a one-floor, cinder-block garage with a pull-down gate. Inside the garage would be two half-ton pick-up trucks with "AEIOU REFRIGERATION REPAIR" stenciled on the front doors. I could see myself in front of the place with overalls. It was a good, solid, satisfying picture, something worth working toward. Amy let me off in front of a Gap.

"Remember," she said as the cab was about to speed away, "classes commence at noon tomorrow. Don't fuck it up."

I purchased the best pair of overalls in the place. I looked really good in them, and inspected myself in the mirror awhile until the sales-chick said, "Will that be all?"

While walking around I found a pair of sunglasses and a rainbow-colored headband that complemented the overalls. Soon I meandered home. I located a large claw hammer and admired myself in the mirror. I was born to wear overalls and swing a hammer. It was early afternoon, and she was still at work, so I went to sleep in the overalls, still clenching the hammer.

My growling stomach woke me up: hunger. Amy still wasn't home. In the kitchen cabinet, everything had been thrown out except bouillon cubes, tomato paste, and Saltines. I mixed these together in a small pot, added a little warm water, steamed it, and ate it down. It wasn't so bad.

CHAPTER TEN
TRUTH IS WHAT WORKS

A s I went out that night the G-man followed me. I walked around, went to various discount stores, and spent all the money Amy had given me on petty indulgences, entirely forgetting about the rubber gloves and funnel. I decided to forgo the Downtown scene that night in order to be with my pretty woman. When I got home, though, around midnight, I was broke and starving. My little woman was fast asleep. I awoke my woman.

"Come to bed," she grogged. "You've got your first class tomorrow." She then rolled over and went back to sleep. I shook her again.

"What?" she bolted up when I touched her.

"Can you spare any change?" I said delicately. "I'm genuinely starving."

"My god, is there no escaping beggars in this city? I worked a ten-hour day, and sacrificed my lunch hour to get you a livelihood. Can't I sleep in peace?"

"You're my girlfriend. You owe me."

"Pardon me?"

"If it wasn't for you, I'd still have a job proofreading."

"How much do you want?" She reached over to her purse.

"I'd like three hundred a week."

"What?"

"That's how much I used to gross proofreading."

"I'll loan you the money until you are employed as a refrigeration technician. Then I expect to get it all back." I agreed.

"Do you want me to sign some kind of agreement?" I asked.

"You're my boyfriend, I trust you," she said in a strange tone. She took fifty out of her purse and laid back down.

"While you're awake and it's still night, let's have sex," I said, hoping to seize an opportunity. She didn't reply, she just lay there.

I inspected her more closely. She had gone to sleep. Sex was always the first thing to go in a relationship; fighting was the last thing to go. I took the fifty and went out. The G-man's car was across the street. I tried hailing a cab, but there were none. I went to the G-man, opened the rear door of his car, and got in.

"Can you take me to the Nuyorican Poet's Cafe? They're having a poetry slam."

"Get the hell out of my Buick," he said without turning around.

"You're following me. Why don't we just do it this way?"

"Get out of my car. I'm waiting for my wife."

I got out and successfully hailed a cab to the Nuyorican Poet's Cafe to hear some poetry of our age. The G-Man followed. I paid my five bucks at the door and went up to the bar. The slam apparently was already over, people were drinking and mingling. I saw the G-Man peeking inside, looking for me. My new body really made a difference. Finding a roll of black masking tape, I taped a little on my chin so it looked like a plastic goatee.

Moving around, I bought a beer at a usurious price, then came on to as many girls as I could. Finally, I approached one cute chick and introduced myself as last week's poetry slam champ. I showed her ten bucks, the prize money, as proof. She couldn't have been much older than sixteen. We talked about TV shows. I finally won her over with my crisp recollections of the early '80s, and she let me buy her a beer.

"So you write poetry?" I asked as if I cared.

"I'm working on a long poem about sleazy guys who'll say anything to get laid, how 'bout you?"

"What are the roots that clutch?" I said in a fierce and demonic tone. "What branches grow, out of this stony rubbish? Son of man, you cannot say or guess, for you know, only a heap of broken images where the sun beats, the dead tree gives no shelter, the cockroach no relief, but there is shadow under this red rock. Come in under the red rock of my apartment and I'll show you your shadow at morning striding behind you or your shadow at evening striding to meet you. I'll show you fear in a handful of dust..."

"Your red rock needs a little work," she replied.

"What kind of work?" It was part of Eliot's *The Wasteland*.

"It needs, like, a victim, or someone we can feel bad for. Like an oppressed group or something."

I steered the conversation away from modern poetry and careened her to the balcony where our lips collided in kisses. I touched her here and there and then nodded off. When I was awakened a couple hours later, I was alone. It was morning. I went out and tried to hail a cab, but there were none on B and Third. I saw the G-man and got in the back seat of his car.

"Home, Jeeves."

"My name's not Jeeves. Get the hell out of my car. I'm waiting for my wife."

I got out of his car and slowly walked along Second, from Avenue B to Avenue A. He followed twenty feet behind me the entire time, until I finally got a cab on First Avenue, and we went home.

As soon as I opened the door to my apartment, I saw a big sign waiting for me. It read, "WHERE ARE YOU? FIRST CLASS IS TODAY AT NOON, DON'T FUCK UP!!"

It was 7:00 in the morning. I could comfortably catch four

hours of sleep and get there by noon. I rummaged around a bit and looked through the remains of my collections that had been stocked into boxes—all my old copies of underground magazines and journals such as the *SoHo Weekly News*, the *East Village Eye*, and the *Berkeley Barb* were gone. Also gone were my anthologies of *Celebrity Skin*, featuring Hollywood Starlets when they were just high-priced call girls, and my rare "Warts and Farts" issues of *Hustler*. I lay down in a slight daze and dozed off. I woke to the ring of the telephone.

"How was it?"

"How was what?" I said drowsily. "Who is this? Where am I?"

"Your girlfriend, asshole."

"My girlfriend's what?"

"This is your girlfriend, asshole." It was Amy: I loved her. "How was your first class?" I looked at the clock, it was 5:00 p.m.

"It was first class!"

"What did you learn?"

"We got a breakdown of conventional refrigeration appliances," I lied unimaginatively. "Today's focus, though, was on conventional home-style stand-ups."

"Like what?"

"Like G.E., Westinghouse, Maytag…"

"What exactly did you learn?"

"Well…" I was out of material. Refrigerators didn't inspire me.

"Yes?" She wouldn't relent.

"You know those little magnets with the little fruits on one side."

"What about them?"

"They're…ummm."

"They're what?"

"They're poison to your standard home machine rheometers, especially the large-fruit magnets."

"Large fruit magnets?"

"Yeah, like cantaloupe and watermelon magnets. They usually have two magnet strips behind them."

"Where did you end up purchasing your specially treated funnel?"

"Small place near the river called Mesticles," I quickly invented. "It sounds like you're cross-examining me!"

"You're lying!" She switched gears into a holler, "I received a call five minutes ago from your guidance counselor who informed me that you missed your first class!"

"Did you throw out my archives of underground journals?!" My first day and I was already assigned a guidance counselor.

"I certainly did and I don't want to even talk about them."

"But..."

"But don't worry," she added. "We will have a talk. Don't go anywhere, I'm coming home right now." She then hung up.

Oy, what was I going to say? She caught me red-handed. A moment later, she entered. "Now what the hell is going on? Either you provide me with a reasonable explanation, or this relationship is *finis*."

"You want an explanation!" I began confidently, seeming to launch into a strong retort, but actually blank-minded. I began giving a brief history of the nature of consciousness, talking about the Great Earth Mother and the heroic evolution of the ego, and how the great egoless ego was symbolized by a snake swallowing its own tail.

"What!" she screamed like a swooping bird. The scream snatched a marooned thought in its talons, and I was suddenly on to something else.

"I feel a complete lack of faith in you," I said, "and it's paralyzed me."

"What are you talking about?"

"Sex! This is supposed to be a sexual relationship, but we haven't even seen each other nude! Explain that to me!" Amy started coughing. She coughed for such a length of time, I dashed to the kitchen and fetched some water in a bowl. After drinking it, she asked, "What do I look like, a cat?" The bowl was the only thing that was clean.

"You okay?"

"I'm coming down with laryngitis," she rasped. "You're giving it to me!"

"Before you lose your voice, explain to me how you're always so carefully out of the house when I'm excited, and vice versa?" If there was a vice versa.

"I..."

"Tell me what man would tolerate this behavior!"

"What are you talking about?"

"Sex! Why don't we have sex?!"

"Fine, have sex if you must."

"I mean with each other."

"How does this relate to you not having gone to class?"

"I'm drawing on your strength is how! And that strength isn't coming because I don't believe you care for me!"

"Well...well..." she sputtered.

I had found a breach and wasn't about to acquiesce. I was on the offensive. In point of fact, I was sick of her You-can't-make-an-omelet-without-breaking-eggs attitude, and I saw quite realistically that there was little chance this relationship was going to float very long. Too quickly, she was spotting cracks in my hull. It was time to find the best life boat and abandon ship.

"Well?!" I asked with a false indignation.

"All right?" she interrupted. "You're right, I do love you, but I have something painful to tell you first."

"What?"

"I can't make love to you until...until you get the pupil-fusion operation. I can't bear looking into your eyes."

"Why? What's the big deal about the color of my eyes?"

"I can still see the old monster staring at me through those eyes."

"I'll wear sunglasses."

"No, we can have the operation done tomorrow. It only

takes twenty minutes. The optometrist assured me there's no risk."

"What is this operation exactly?"

"Did you ever see David Bowie in *The Man Who Fell to Earth?* Where they fuse the pupils to his eyes? It's like that."

"I didn't see it, but I'll do it."

"When it's done, we'll consummate our love."

That night we slept nervously. She kept coughing, and I kept thinking how this was the last night that my eyes would be their natural hazel.

By the next day, the laryngitis had completely consumed her. With a cup of Hazelnut coffee and a warmed croissant, she quietly informed me that it was time to get up. She had awakened hours earlier and managed to secure a morning appointment with the noted eye-butcher, Dr. Mort Slocum. I dressed. Amy accompanied me, probably to be certain I wouldn't run off. While in the waiting room of his attractive, ground-floor office on Fifth Avenue, I gained faith from his selection of quality, updated magazines that he was a good doctor.

We sat in the waiting area across from each other. There was only one other patient, a middle-aged woman who looked like the mother I never had, voluptuous under a business outfit, buried behind a copy of *Mademoiselle*.

If safe sex required any kind of patience and conviction, it was nothing compared to what I was about to undergo. Soon, the doctor came out and shook my hand, saying he was delighted to see me. He told me it was just a quick piece of cosmetic surgery, and gave me photos of before-and-after cases who underwent the operation. The "befores" were frowning, the "afters" were smiling. Other than that, I saw no difference. Then he excused himself to go to the bathroom.

"Don't forget to scrub your hands," I called out to him. Rushing over to Amy, I appealed, "Can't I just get a cheap feel to keep me motivated while I'm in there under the doctor's knife?"

"It's not a knife. It's a laser beam."

"That's even worse!"

Looking at me, she tightened her face like a fist, and through gritting teeth she hissed, "Okay, go ahead, feel it! Grope it!"

I told her that I'd wait till after the operation. The doctor returned and told me to follow him.

"There's something I want to say before I go," I said to Amy.

"What?"

"Remember how, before Gorbachev, the U.S. and Russia had enough weapons to destroy the world, and each of the other's weapons were pointed into the heart of the other, how that created great distrust, but kept the other on each other's minds to the point of constant, day-to-day anxiety?"

"Yeah."

"It wasn't like a big country dominating a little country, and it wasn't like two big, dumb countries at constant peace, was it?"

"No, the doctor's waiting for you."

"It was two big countries with huge and sophisticated weaponry pointed directly at each other, and both countries were stuck on the same globe."

"So?"

"A generation of drills, school children under the table, backyard bomb shelters, the birth of bottled water..."

"So?"

"It was adversarial polarity."

"So?"

"I, too, have developed an adversarial polarity for you."

"Huh?"

"Mr. Aeiou," Sawbones Slocum called, "I get paid by the hour. Let's paint those pupils, shall we?"

"What I'm trying to say is I'm animus possessed!" I explained.

"Huh?"

"I love you," I replied, employing the colloquial term. Then the strangest thing occurred: I distinctly saw the swell of a tear in Amy's cold, functional eyes.

"I'm sorry about everything," she replied and kissed me. Despite the laryngitis, she assured me that she would be there waiting for me when I got out. I followed the doctor into the examination room.

CHAPTER ELEVEN
'DON'T DIS YOUR SIS'

D r. Mortimer Slocum reassured me that although the operation was new and difficult, it was a quick procedure, and he'd have me out of there in twenty minutes tops.

"There are no side effects or anything?"

"Why, are you a lawyer?"

"No."

"Just stay home for a couple days and for god's sake, don't take off the cotton patches until tomorrow afternoon."

"What patches?"

"You'll have to keep your eyes patched until tomorrow." He then called in a nurse. Together we went into a small room where I was laid back. He looked into my eyes, placed the soft plastic lenses, and inserted what felt like a tiny, red-hot poker into each eyeball. I felt a blinding light.

As a strobe of light zapped my cones and rods, I remembered Byzantine Emperor Basil II. Upon capturing fifteen thousand Bulgarian troops, he had them blinded, leaving every hundredth man with one eyeball in order to lead the rest of them back to their homeland.

Why was I doing this? I wondered. Then I remembered. My reagan pup-tented in my pants as I fantasized having sex with Amy while the procedure was done to the other eye. Then he applied bandages.

He excused himself, departed, and in a moment, Amy was there before me.

"Did it hurt, my little bat?" she hissed and rattled. The laryngitis had pulverized her voice.

"Excruciating, my little snake," I replied, placing the guilt-ridden foundations upon her to support the sexual colossus I was hoping to build. As she led me outside and into a cab, I started slipping my hand down her buttoned blouse.

"Don't you want to wait," she whispered, "until you can see?"

"I'll see feelingly." I borrowed Shakespeare for the occasion. An eternity passed as she paid the cabby and we fumbled up the stairs. I rubbed up against her with every step. As she grappled for her key, I groped at her. By the time I heard the door slam, my reagan was ready for its own performance of *Bedtime For Bonzo*.

"Hold it!" she whispered, fighting her sore larynx. "I'm not nearly as experienced at this as you are, Bundles. I've only had sex three times, and I don't want this to be any cheaper than it is."

"Too late," I replied, and rushed her.

"Hold it!" she said. "If we really have to do it like this, at least let me get a drink."

"All right, get me one, too!"

I heard her go off to the kitchen and in a moment she returned with two glasses and a bottle. We drank our swill quickly. Then I battled her, bathed in her, drank her, nipped and nibbled her, all mere foreplay. Her clothes restrained and disguised her true resources. Before long, she appealed for a second bottle of vodka.

Over the next hour or so, a lot of alcohol was ingested in small, slippery quantities, and in the bathroom I felt my way through the medicine chest for some lewd quaaludes that I had from long ago. Soon she was as smooth as silk, soft as a pat of butter, and loose as a goose. But in another moment she started sinking into sleep. She couldn't say a word, just a bunch of gurgling sounds. I finally placed her on the bed and wormed my way up that list of psycho-sexual fantasies like a rectal suppository. A couple times she would moan in pain, and her consciousness would peek out from the shroud of intoxication as she appealed for the traditional positions that were a part of her family values.

"Nonsense," I retorted. "Moral sex is banal sex."

On and on we went, the hunter and hunted, like a nation buying joy it never earned, spending money it never had. At one point, feeling like a teenager, I gave a sensuous hickey just above her breast. Eventually she passed out, and after a couple more hours of unilateral adversarial pole-arising (a/k/a lovemaking), so did I.

The next day, late in the afternoon, I awoke to the sound of the shower. I carefully peeled off my eye patches, and my eyes slowly adjusted. Checking my blue eyes in the mirror, I discovered that I finally had something in common with Paul Newman and Frank Sinatra. I fuzzily remembered almost everything from last night. I went to my half of the house and did some pore inspection. Then she came out of the bathroom, entered my part of the house, and looked at me strangely.

"What's the matter, my turtle dove?"

"What did you do to me last night?"

"Whatever do you mean? We made love."

"YOU DISGUSTING PIG!!" she suddenly shrieked. "Oh god, how could I delude myself so miserably? You're even more disgusting than you were before!"

"What do you mean, my love?"

She stormed out, back to her apartment. I trailed after her, but she'd locked the door. When I returned to my apartment, I wondered what the problem was and how much money it would cost to rectify. My devotion to Amy was the most sobering path I had ever walked, and I didn't want to lose it. Suddenly my phone, which few had the number to, rang.

"He doesn't live here or want any," I answered, hoping to fend off tele-sellers and wrong numbers.

"I got photos of you with a piece of tape on your chin feeling up some thirteen-year-old girl at the Nuyorican Poet's Cafe." It was Whitlock.

"What?"

"And I just want you to know, sleazebag, that it wasn't your looks and charms that did it. We paid her to let you." So that G-man did some work the other night.

"Hah." I feigned a one-note chuckle.

"They're in the mail to Amy. Let's see how you talk yourself out of this one."

"She knows all about it, asshole. You think you can extort our relationship to death? Forget it! We have an open, honest relationship. A simple relationship that takes into account the dynamic excursions of the male libido." I hung up the phone. That fucking thirteen-year-old hadn't looked a day younger than fifteen.

The phone rang a moment later. Him: "Look, I give up. Just say it. Dictate your terms. What do you want to stay out of my life and leave me and Amy alone forever?"

"Nothing." I hung up the phone, he called back. I had no intention of parting with Amy, but I remembered the determination that Whitlock used when he called me after the stand-up comedy episode at *YUK!*, so I decided to make him an offer that he would refuse.

"I want cash, cold and hard and green. And a lot of it."

"How much?"

"Three hundred and fifty-seven thousand dollars, and thirty-eight cents."

"WHAT!"

"That's my price, and I'll never see her again."

"You're crazy!"

"That has nothing to do with it."

"I ain't giving you a cent. I can hire some college kid to kill you for a thousand bucks, pal."

"Sure you can. But even dead she'll be mine. Morrison, Elvis, and Jim Croce all reached greater heights of popularity in death than in their lives. She'll be my number one Elvis impersonator, pal."

"I'll give you half of that."

"Fuck that. You're rich. In fact, get me back into the masters program, reinstate me in the proofreading agency, and come up with four hundred and eighty-two thousand dollars and twenty-eight cents."

"Hey, I'm willing to compromise in the middle."

"The meter's running, pal. Now, I'm looking at my watch; you got ten seconds to make up your mind." I silently counted to five and then hung the phone up. Just as quickly, it rang again.

"Okay, I'll do it!" He wasn't supposed to accept the offer. I hung up the phone in a panic.

I ran into the bathroom and locked the door. I had no idea what to do. I was terrible at confrontation, even with my big, new body. I still reverted to a seven-year-old when in fear. I jumped in the bathtub and covered my eyes so he couldn't see me. Through the wall, though, I could hear Amy wildly weeping in her apartment. Last night's intimacy had been too much for her, poor kid.

I went to the green door and tried knocking softly. I really did love her. I wasn't aware that I had done anything wrong. But even I am capable of some guilt. I kept reminding myself that whatever kind of violation I might have unintentionally performed, she, with her unauthorized series of zip-lock operations, had made me look like an amateur, even if they were an improvement. But I felt incredibly guilty. It must have been a sacrifice for her to miss one of those power lunches to find me a blue-collar vocational skill. I gently knocked on Amy's door.

"I'll kill you, you pig. Stay away from that door."

"Let's put this behind us."

Like a promising act at CBGBs, I could hear her violent shrieks to the accompaniment of explosive glassware. Suddenly there was a knock at my front door. Through the peephole, I saw him, the unshelled nut. I turned up the TV to blanket all sounds from her room and opened my door. He was holding his extra-thin briefcase. He meant business.

"Christ, can you lower that?" *My Favorite Martian* was blaring.

"Afraid not, pal. It drowns out the voices in my head."

Using his knee as a desk, he set down his briefcase and unclicked it open. WOW! I seized a tightly ribboned stack of hundred dollar bills. It looked genuine with a capital G. He handed it to me—mine! For a moment I lost myself. I asked him to wait in the hall and transferred all the cash into the compartment under the toilet. I had to have it. I wouldn't even spend it, I could just look at it and masturbate. I opened the door again. He was still there expectantly.

"All right, you want her?" I asked, preoccupied with how I was going to sell Amy, who I loved, who hated me, to this man (who hated me), whom she disliked.

"No, I just wanted to see what you'd do with a half-a-million bucks." He wasn't even good at sarcasm.

"All right, look, I'm going to stage a scene. Just play along. Do what comes natural."

"Huh?"

I lowered the TV and went back to the adjoining green door, the Glinika Bridge where the former East Berlin met the former West Berlin of our former relationship. I started banging. "Open this fucking door!" I screamed. "My reagan's at attention and you're my first lady."

"Uruuuugh!" she screamed.

"You arch slime-bag!" he said. Rushing over, he punched me in the back.

"Get off me, you preppie boy!" I shoved him into a pile of boxes that collapsed to one side. The common door opened.

She had heard the commotion and bit the bait. She watched for a minute as I struggled to contain the Terminator-Whitlock. I kept whispering to him things like, "enough," and "quit," and "uncle." But he kept punching, and it really hurt.

"Enough!" she called, as she walked through my half of the house out the front door. She went downstairs carrying a small overnight bag.

"Give me my money back, asshole!"

"No way," I replied calmly. He punched me hard in the nose.

"Punch me, kick me, chew me, kill me. I finally got you, and there's no way I'm going to separate with that cash. My life is worth much less than it, so you'll have to kill me to get it."

"I don't kill people, I hire others to kill them."

He pushed me down and raced around my side of the apartment, searching for his unearned cash. It was already pretty emptied out, but he turned over the few boxes I had. I didn't mind much until he started tossing around my newly purchased clothes. In my kitchen, everything was already near barren; I had no food, one pot, one pan, and one plate. Rushing into the bathroom, he tossed all my skin-care products into the garbage while emptying the medicine cabinet. He still couldn't find it. Then, exhausted, frantic, truly undone and defeated, he raced out the door.

As I heard them storming down the stairs, I rose and went into her half of the house, where I flushed the blood out of my nose and held a compress up to my eyes. They were still recovering from yesterday's operation, and my sight was blurry as I inspected her half of the apartment. It was designed in a classical Grecian manner, like a temple yet to be despoiled. There was a sunken waterway set in faux marble.

When I got to her bedroom I found the true riches of her place. She had an entire room devoted to television. It was loaded with different cable boxes and three thirty-inch sets, side by side, positioned before a non-impact treadmill. Flipping through the different channels I realized that besides MTV and VH1, she had the Comedy Channel, and to top it all off, the Playboy Channel. She had four different movie channels! *FOUR!*

I tallied the score. On the down side, I had lost my great love, my adversarial pole. On the plus side, though, I had a half-renovated palace. I had a half-renovated set of looks— my true "ugliness," as Amy pointed out, was still intact, and I'd only be able to fool chicks until they got a full taste of my character. Most importantly, I had nearly half-a-million bucks. Not a bad jump on life.

Slowly, over the next couple of hours, as I regained the full power of sight, I realized my new purpose in life. I'd spend the rest of my days preparing, cultivating, and hopefully winning the other half of everything.

I sat down and started watching the multiple TV sets simultaneously. It was wonderful, all these scantily clothed, bouncy chicks. I went to her fridge and found a plate of tasty-looking hors d'oeuvres, which I brought over to the TV room. The Robert Palmer video was on, the one with all those leggy, look-a-like chicks in black miniskirts. I watched the legs and wolfed down the delicious little foods and fell asleep. But it wasn't working. All the girls in Robert Palmer's video were Amy. The food was Amy. The hi-tech comforts were all Amy. I fell asleep dreaming about Amy.

When I awoke, it was a couple hours later. One of my many viruses was with me, the dull fever. That fever was Amy. Hoping to displace my obsessive love for Amy with money, I took some cash and went out into the street. With money, it was a new and different street. I had to buy something. I was weak and hungry, so I went to the nearest restaurant.

I visited Graceland once, and in the same way that Elvis Presley had all the best of the worst objects, I went to a McDonald's and ordered everything on the menu. Everything, sparing nothing. I ordered it all to go, in every size—small, medium, and large—and in all varieties: salads, fries, burgers, cheese burgers, Big Macs, Quarter Pounders, hot fruit pies—everything in bags. One of the girls was wearing a belt with a neat "M" insignia on it. For some feverish reason, I knew Amy would like it.

"Can I buy that from you?" I asked the cashier, pointing to her waist.

"Screw you."

"No, the belt."

"My belt?"

"Yeah, I'll give you ten bucks for it. It's for Amy."

"No thanks."

I pulled out twenty bucks.

"All right." She gave me her belt. As she turned around to pull the belt off discreetly, I noticed the golden arches insignia on the back of her pants. Amy would want this to go with her new belt.

"Do you want to sell me your pants?"

"For a hundred bucks I will."

I didn't want them that much, which meant Amy would probably want them, since her tastes were the opposite of mine. I gave the cashier a hundred dollar bill, took her belt and all the food I could carry, and got back some change.

At first I gorged myself, but I heard it. I whipped around, looking for her, and munched again. Again I heard it: Amy was saying, "Take mouth-size bites. Chew slowly. Let the food digest."

Finally though, I realized Amy would not appreciate this purchase. I looked down at the tightly packaged food that hollered, EAT ME! I pushed the bundled food away, but became aware that people were looking at me, giving me that people-are-starving look. I spent awhile on a french fry. But I could taste the sugar laced throughout it; it was like eating poison. I started sweating profusely and getting itchy. EAT ME! commanded the food. Someone leaving held the door open a moment. Hopping to my feet, I dashed out and to the corner. Fearing I was being chased like at *YUK!*, I dashed down into a subway hole, over the turnstile, and into an awaiting subway train. As the doors closed I realized that although no one was behind me, Amy was the fever in my head. My eyes were seeing double Amy in baby blue.

I consulted silently with her for a moment. We were rich! It was like we were chosen to live! We could do anything we wanted. We could have people killed if they forced us to eat fast food. We could do serious crimes and get off easily in country clubs. We danced on the subway and felt lightheaded. Life felt heavenly, like a wonderful interpretation of death. Indeed, for the first time I didn't hunger for death.

A bunch of people were sitting quietly in their seats behaving themselves. As far as a bunch of people went, they seemed docile. They appeared hardworking. They were a fair slice of New York. All races, sexes, and ages were well represented. They were what we loved about New York, and we felt sorry for their plight, having to take the subways every day. As New Yorkers, they had suffered so that the rest of the country could delude itself into believing it was healthier, happier, and safer. They deserved something for this punishment.

We got up in the center of the car and announced, "Excuse us, ladies and gentleman. We don't mean to be a pain but we're a well-educated white man and his well-educated white girlfriend. We didn't go to Vietnam and we have all our limbs and we don't have any ailments and we live together in a large, comfy Upper East Side apartment and have a lot to be thankful for. If anybody needs any spare change, please just tell us how much, and we'll try to oblige you. Remember, any idiot can become rich. Thank you."

One guy laughed insanely. The other commuters completely ignored us. But as we neared the end of the subway car, one fashionable young man with a hook in his face asked me if we could spare a five for a flick. We informed him that it cost more than that but gave it to him anyway. Then we gave him six bucks more for popcorn.

"Hey, you got a hundred bucks?" someone said next. Amy said to give him only twenty, so we gave a twenty.

"Do you have fifty?" a lady asked. Amy gave her a five.

"Hey! Give me a dollar," some old lady screamed from across the train. She came over and I gave it to her.

"Amy and I hope you live a happy life," I said for both of us.

"What are you, crazy?" she said as she seized the bill out of our hands. "You're all alone."

And so, in *The Epic of Gilgamesh* it is written, "What you seek you will never find." Happiness was a mere delusion of having both Amy and money. The old lady's comment twisted through my sternum like a rusty corkscrew and tugged out my greasy heart. I stood there alone, Amyless.

The entire car-full of people were moving toward me like an army of zombies, no longer the noble people of New York. They were pushy at rush hour, intervening when something was a bargain, neglectful when someone needed help. As the door opened at the next stop, I dashed out and up.

I had lost track of the subway track and was up in Harlem. I walked among the locals looking for alternate transportation. On one corner, I noticed a well-behaved line of people buying drugs. Police spotters were on each end of the street, and there was a dealer in the middle of the block. I got at the end of the jittery-yet-mannered cue. When my turn came, I asked for a nickel bag.

"A nickel what? Who are you? Fuck off!"

"Look, you have to sell it to me!"

"Fuck away! Get out of here whiteboy before I blow you away!"

As a visual aide, he took out a cheap handgun and pointed it in my face.

"Shoot, go ahead. Life is worth nothing without my her. I'm Aimless without Amy." Her life was probably joyful without me—Joey.

162

"Get out of here." He smacked my sore nose with the flat of the cheap handgun.

"Ow!" The pain gave me an idea. "Hey, how much would it cost for you to shoot someone? I'll give you ten thousand dollars."

"Bring the money and we'll talk."

"Here." I flashed three hundred dollars in his ratty face.

"Shit!" He grabbed at my money. I pulled away, he chased, I raced.

"Grab that little shit!"

One of the spotters cut me off and held my arms behind my back. The dealer went through my pockets and took out all my money, three hundred and twelve dollars and twenty-eight cents. He took the three hundred and put the twelve and change back in my shirt pocket.

"Now beat it."

"Keep the cash but give me the gun, and I won't call the police."

"Okay," he said complacently. "Here, I guess it's better than killing you and going to jail for six years. And if you do call the police, I'll have you arrested for having a concealed weapon." Clever, he must have been a lawyer before dealing drugs.

As I walked over to 125th Street, I inspected the gun. It looked convincing, but there was only one way to tell. I pointed the weapon in the air and pulled the trigger. A screw fell out of the handle, but nothing fast came out of the front. I clicked the gun into the air repeatedly, and not entirely without results. A cabby, thinking I was hailing, came to a halt. I took it home. The ride was rough and circuitous. But like everyone else in this city, even with the gun, I was too afraid to give the maniac a punitively small tip.

CHAPTER TWELVE

PUT YOUR HAND IN SHIT AND YOU'LL GET SHIT ON YOUR HAND

Amy," I whispered into the fuzziness of the night, "where art thou?" Nothing answered articulately. I turned on all the TVs, all to MTV, but it did no good. The libido was not libiding while Amy was out there. Love was great and pure, and I could never love or even think of another woman.

Locating a small envelope of coke, I did a line and sleaze-bang! Ma'ams, madames, ms', and misses. Lips thin or ample, barrels of kisses. Oodles and noodles of Chinese Chix! Gals, ladies, getting kicks. A sultan's harem of sultry lasses. Girls with soft contacts, girls in glasses. Kittens and nymphs, hot sensations. Aproned matrons in tight formations. Parades, parodies, endless cavalcades. Brat packs in slacks, mistresses, maids. Anorectics, bulimics, and round pound rolleys. Thinking mamas like Cher or Jane Trudeau Pauley. Babes flowing, strutting, a wide-open faucet. Quiet gals, brainy, with skeletons in closet. Babs: Walters, Streisand; and Sue: Sommers, Saint James. Tall, small mall chicks, those with no names. Downtown-scene chicks, dirty and clean chicks, teens-in-jeans chicks, shallow and deep chicks, fiscal and leap...

But when the drug passed: Amy, amy, amyamyamy yam my amy may may am ama ma mama ay.... I fell asleep.

I woke up early the next day. I missed the breakfast special by six hours, so I got a jelly donut and coffee at the counter of a local diner. While walking toward my door, I became bookended between two massive men.

"Thought I'd find you here," said one. Looking up, I reconized that guy Wylie, who had served me the macaroni and cheese at Whitlock's house. I tried to leap backward, but he already had his hand on my back. So did the other guy, some thug-for-hire.

"Do you remember me?" he inquired politely.

"Yeah, you're the guy that talks to himself. If you're going to beat me or kill me for the money, forget it. I spent it. But if you want, you can kill me anyway. Just let me see my old apartment one last time." I was hoping to get hold of the cheap handgun and kill them.

"What? Hell no. I'm just sorry if I behaved strangely the first time we met."

"Oh no, I'm amused by stream-of-consciousness types."

"Well, this time I'm prepared to speak in the traditional, dialogical fashion. Whitlock would kill me if he knew I was here talking to you."

"So do us both a favor and…"

"You're having an important birthday soon, so you have to know!" Wylie shot back.

"What do you want? I have money!"

"Shut up, just listen a minute." He paused for a moment and then launched, "Suppose…Suppose…Suppose…Help me, Herman!"

"How?" Herman asked.

"Suppose you heard about this poor guy…" Wylie began.

"Yeah, a guy…" Herman echoed.

"And he was the son of an old cow."

"An old cow? You're calling Mister…an old cow?" exclaimed Herman.

"I mean…a lion…" Wylie revised.

"A lion?" I asked.

"Yeah, he was a lion cub…but he was told he was a messy, skinny chicken." When we arrived at my apartment, they indicated that I could take out my key and enter the front door.

"Yeah, a lion cub that's a chicken," uttered Herman as if it all made perfect sense.

"A guy is a lion cub, but he thinks he's a chicken?" I asked.

"YES!" Wylie yelled impatiently.

"Fine."

"Bear with us, Joey." Wylie fell silent for a moment, searching for more components of this bizarre, bestial tale.

"Well?" Herman finally asked Wylie.

"Well," Wylie said, "how would that little lion cub feel if he realized that all his life he was treated like a creepy little chicken?"

"Crappy?" I guessed, sensing that somehow I was going to be equated to that chicken lion cub. But by the time we got to my inner door, I still couldn't figure out how.

"What I'm trying to say is…"

"No!" Herman stopped him. "You can't tell him nothing more!"

"But…"

"If you do, we're both dead! You know that," Herman said.

"You're right," Wylie responded, and added, "Kid, you've got to figure it out from there." Without further explanation of their fable, they turned and left. Aesop they weren't.

The Amy craving was still there. I tried calling her at work, but I hung up. I called information and then the American Psychiatric Association to inform them that to be honest to their reclining public, love had to be officially listed as a psychosis. They hung up on me.

The next day, I pursued puerile pastimes. I took the Circle Line. That evening I saw a play at Circle in the Square. Afterwards, I ate at La Cirque, which somehow reminded me of a circus.

I went home, and while thinking of how to spend my new

life, I watched music videos. In the same way that the '60s brought us the space program, music videos were the '80s' contribution to mankind. The phone rang. Not my phone, her phone. I answered.

"Oh, I'm sorry. I must have the wrong number," the female said, and hung up.

The phone rang again. This time I raised my voice a couple of octaves, put my hand over the speaker, and said in a raspy voice, "Hello."

"Amy?"

"I've got laryngitis. Identify yourself, quickly."

"This is Sophie. I'm just calling to find out when the big event is going to be."

"Oh, I'm sorry. You have the wrong Amy," I said and hung up. The conversation made everything tumble forth for me. What big event could she be referring to? My whole life was built around loving or hating her; I couldn't withdraw. Another paradox of love is that the lover (dispeller of love) wants to use the lovee (the victim of love) as a physical and emotional toilet, wherein one can flush a variety of messy longings, freaky fantasies, and pathetic needs. If someone really loved someone else, they'd stay the hell away from them. Unfortunately for Amy, I didn't love her enough to stay away from her. If she ever really did find her way to loving someone like me then something deep inside of her still loved me. (I don't know why I knew this, I just did.)

The only way to get the love bug out of your system is by rendering it commonplace, through overexposure. Reconciliation would be the best thing for both of us. This would require: a) seeing her apart from the monster Whitlock, b) somehow showing her that my illogical state was due to the operations (my ego attack had given me an acute case of selfishness, but I had managed to regain my senses), c) proving my undying love for her (I might be able to pull that all off, but by far the hardest thing to do would be d)), and d) convincing her that her love for me, although fugitive from her consciousness, was still very alive, and not delusional.

I didn't know where she was staying but I knew where she worked. I dialed her number, "I'd like to speak to Miss Rapapport."

"I'm sorry, Miss Rapapport is unavailable."

"Why?"

"She's simply unavailable."

I hung up. It was quite clear what had happened. The lady who called, Sophie, said it. The "big event" was going to happen. Amy had finally consented to marrying the Whitlock monster. This must have killed her drive to make stacks of money because no matter how brilliant or lucky she was, she would never be able to compete with the money she would marry into. But this would also kill all her purpose in life! Didn't she know that? It would be just a Mme. Bovary revisited, couldn't she see that? I had to prevent the marriage. Over the past week or so I had discovered that money was not the means to ultimate happiness; I knew that only Amy could bring me that. Since he had Amy, since he had everything, my mission was clear: I had to kill him. I picked up the phone and called him.

"Whitlock Incorporated," said the horse-eyed receptionist.

"Yes, my name is Wilbur Whitlock, and I..."

"Oh no, I was warned about you. You stop calling here. Shoo!" She hung up. I dialed back.

"Hello," I said in a brogue. "This is Father Dorris, and I'm supposed to conduct..."

"We know who you are, and we'll notify the police if you don't stop calling this instant." She hung up again.

It was still daytime. I raced over to the rhombus-shaped building and waited in the cavernous lobby. The layout of the place, with the overhead mezzanine filled with security guards and the docile inmate-employees, reminded me of a minimum security prison—a day prison. And these were the day people. They were dormant in their homes at night and activated here by day. When the elevator opened, some suits got out. One suit in particular had the word "day" written all over him—he was pure rank and file. I followed him out into the street.

"Excuse me," I said to the suit.

"Yes?"

"Do you work at Whitlock Incorporated?"

"Yes."

"Do you know Mr. Andrew Whitlock?"

"Yes."

"Was he out today?"

"Yes."

"Would you know if he's getting married?"

"Yes."

"Is he getting married?"

"No."

"Does the name Amy Rapapport ring a bell?"

"No."

"Do you know if he's romantically attached to anyone?"

"No," the day-suit concluded. Then he began asking a few questions: "What is it you want?"

"A girl named Amy Rapapport."

"Have you tried the phone book?"

"No."

"You thought she had married Whitlock?"

"Yes."

"Are you a friend of Whitlock's?"

"No."

"Are you rivals for this girl?"

"Yes."

"Well, good luck," he said, and departed before the long, dark, false lashes of evening could batt. I went home and, deciding to take the day-worker's advice, called information and got a phone number for Amy that I vaguely recognized. I dialed it; it rang and rang. I faintly heard a distant ringing and realized that I had dialed the front half of my apartment.

The next morning, I found a letter in the mailbox addressed to Ms. Amy Rapapport. It was from the Bundles O' Joy Adoption Agency. I tore it open and read it:

Dear Ms. Rapapport,
In response to your donation, I have located the requested information on an infant named Joseph, adopted by the family of Ngm. This file is marked "CONFIDENTIAL, refer to Whitlock Incorporated." Please contact the Whitlock Corporation for information on this matter.

Counselor R. LaCosta
Adoption Officer

They had their hands in everything. Stopping at a corner store, I purchased a big bottle of Colt 45 and a "holiday-size" bag of M&Ms (with almonds). When I brought my goods up to the register, I saw a blurry, old jar sitting on the counter. I opened it and took out a long, stringy thing that looked like a very large beef jerky.

"What is that?" asked the cashier.

"Isn't it beef jerky?" I asked nervously.

"Yeah, that's right. It's been so long since anyone opened that thing, I forgot it was even there." Looking at the label, he noticed the price was twenty cents.

"Twenty cents? Wow!" I replied. "I never bought anything that cheap." I took a bite out of it. It tasted like an old belt, but it made a challenging chew so I kept masticating, ingesting, and digesting as I walked home. About halfway through, I decided the jerky both tasted like and was as difficult to eat as an old purse. I returned, depressed, to my apartment, only to find it had been broken into. Whitlock or some ding-a-ling working for him had entered and rustled through my half of the apartment. Nothing appeared to be missing. Still depressed, I watched more MTV videi. I started feeling an intense bellyache, but fortunately I also started feeling irresistibly sleepy.

My dream started out simply enough. I was walking in the woods, but there was a bright light in the sky. A tractor beam lifted me, and I seemed to be a UFO abductee: I was entering into a clean, white room with an eye chart on the wall and a check-up table covered with wax paper. I was wearing a backless patient's robe and was preoccupied with hiding my tushy. A doctor entered. He had Whitlock's face, though he was fat, short, and oily.

"You're a doctor?" I asked.

"I dabble." He looked at my chart, and asked, "When was the last time you had a work-up?"

"What kind of work-up?"

"What's your coverage?" He started surveying my body surface.

"What coverage?"

"What's this?" He was looking at something behind my neck. I put my hand there and quickly located the suspected growth. "That's a pimple. I've been waiting for it to get pointier before picking it. I'm okay," I said. And for some strange reason, I added, "I just need a clean bill of health."

He pushed the cold, flat, circular end of a stethoscope to my chest. "Cough."

I coughed and asked him where he went to medical school.

"Did Hippocrates go to medical school? Did Galileo study physics in high school? Where did Plato study Plato? Experience and soul-searching! I've developed techniques that in a hundred years will become standard practice." He removed a sample-size tube of KY gel from his top drawer. "When were you last inspected for rectal cancer?"

"No way! I don't need a cancer test," I said.

"But I broke the seal on this tube," he replied.

"Tough titty."

"Are there any cancerous predispositions in the family?"

"What do you care?"

"Look, if you're sick, I'm sick."

"Huh?"

Before he could answer me, I morphed into an olive-skinned, turbaned man. I was entering into another room—an office. The phone was ringing. The wall of the office was covered with diplomas commemorating everything: membership in obscure societies, completion of intensive and pedantic courses, cryptic licenses, honors bestowed for unspecified philanthropic services, and titles, including an honorary citizenship in some strange Balkan municipality. Then I noticed that some of the laminated diplomas repeated themselves. Another shelf-laden wall was filled with stone and wooden artifacts from around the world. A network of wooden shelves were covered with fertility symbols, carvings, and hand sculptures—bric-a-brac of all shapes and sizes. A big tom-tom made of a hollowed log was sitting in the corner; behind that, a large, ivory statue of Buddha; and next to that, a brass statuette of the dancing Shiva. On the shelf behind the statuette was a plastic bust of Pope John Paul II. Suddenly, a man in a tacky, plaid suit entered, reading a legal file; again the Whitlock face.

"Scooza mea," I found myself garbling in a strange, indistinguishable dialect. It was apparent that I had only a nominal grasp of English.

"You want a green card, Raj?"

"Yeza, please."

With great difficulty, he tried to navigate the language barrier over the better part of an hour, piloting around strange questions about my life: Whom had I married? How long was I married? What were the sex of my many children? What was my level of education? and so forth.

Finally the sleazy lawyer, Whitlock, asked the unsuspecting illegal alien—me—how much money I had. I smiled elusively and nodded. Again he painstakingly tried to unravel the mystery through primal communication, employing symbols, mime, and dance. Gradually, as it became clear that I was evading an answer, he drew closer and closer, and slowly, in a very nondeliberate way, he started frisking me.

"MONEY!" he said, burning off the last residue of patience. "I NEED MONEY!"

"But vhy?"

"Don't you understand?" he replied. "You are the citizen! I'm the alien! Therefore payment must be made."

The Whitlocker then shoved his hand in my threadbare pants pocket. Dreamy voices awoke me, and I drowned. This time I was intensely young: relentlessly stunning, luminously blonde, awesome blue eyes, a bone structure to end all bone structures. Handsome without compromise. Six-feet-two, one hundred and sixty pounds of rock-hard muscle.

I was in a studio or on a small stage; I was facing rows of empty seats. Through the darkness, in the furthest distance, I saw a poster with intense Svengali eyes penetrating outward. Below it read, THE LÖECHí TECHNIQUE. A slightly stooped Whitlock-mask appeared, *voilà*—he was an acting teacher. A white knit sweater was tied around his shoulders. A tight pair of slacks hugged his heavy midsection and sadly collapsed buttocks. Mascara meticulously struggled to hide his age, a male menopausal make-over. A tastefully colored toupee was carefully anchored into the sideburn hair, which in turn seemed to be woven to his copious ear hairs.

"To learn the coveted secrets of the Löechí will cost you eight hundred American dollars," he said in a slight, untraceable accent.

"What's the Löechí Technique?"

"White light rises from the core of this earth through the kaleidoscope of your feet. It electrifies your spine. We teach harmony, provide you a special water diet, teach you 'exalted movements'…"

"What's so special about this technique?"

"It's movement-based."

"So?"

"It works."

"How do I know it'll work?"

"We ask you to measure your bowel movements. They get longer as your motion gains in majesty." I expected something simple, like sworn testimonials. He showed me sworn scatologicals in a photo album.

"Why do I want my waste any longer? I want to become a successful Hollywood actor." Who doesn't?

"We can't control anyone's destiny. All we can do is give you the tools. Take it or leave it."

"All right, I'll take it." He then moved behind me. Grabbing me around the waist, he started bouncing up and down while yelling, "Jump, Löechí! Jump, Löechí!" I broke away.

"What did you call me?"

"Löechí. You are the Löechí!"

The implements of acting! Green cards of citizenship! A clinical work-up! I struggled up from between the diametric tension of two psycho dream-unweavers: Carl Jung and Joseph Campbell. It all made perfect sense!

One glyph of recollection pulled from the accursed temple of sleep was something Whitlock had muttered about being in Tokyo during the early '60s (probably eluding the Vietnam draft). I quickly upturned all my boxes until I located it, the birth certificate that Amy had located when she first arrived in my apartment. Sure enough, I was made in Japan, right in Tokyo. I was a Tokian while Whitlock was there. I was then adopted by the Ngms. It seemed odd that Amy, who knew everything about Whitlock, wouldn't mention that our paths had crossed in Japan so many years ago. I sniffed a confederate.

Opening a suitcase filled with Amy's stuff, I searched through papers, notebooks, work-related crapola. Flipping through utility bills, unclear warranties, tax-deductible restaurant tabs, a terrifying quantity of metered cab receipts, a copy of my Wittenberg Bible-sized sublease, and so forth, a tiny and much-abused appointment book finally relented, and dropped out.

Thumbing through the book, I saw a listing of appointments. Aerobics were tri-weekly, gynecological appointments were bi-monthly. "Stooges," a client, loomed early in the month, reappeared daily for two weeks like a nervous tic, and then fell off the face of her schedule book—a deal closed. The one cryptic and recurrent staple in her schedule book was a notation that read in capital letters: TOB. It occupied the Tuesday, 7:00 p.m. time slot as if the time were a parcel of real estate. The obvious deduction was that TOB was short for someone named Toby? Tobias? Tabatha? Tobolopolous? A lover she kept? A masseuse she required? A sex club she frequented? Who knew? I flipped through the little pages of her book looking for elaboration of a Toby. None was evident.

Fanning back through the days, weeks, and months, past notions that came and went, I kept encountering that same one: TOB. At last, something yielded. At one time slot, instead of TOB, it read: O. Building. What was the O. Building? I decided to try calling Amy at work and ask her point blank.

I called her office; her secretary picked up.

"Amy, please."

"Yes, who shall I say is calling?"

"I'm calling for the O. Building."

"Yes, who shall I say is calling? Is this you? Is this that sleazy guy I was warned about?"

"Yes. Do you know what the O. Building is?" Very often secretaries are informational run-offs for their basin bosses.

"I was warned about you."

"What is the O. Building?"

"Is this a prank? Are you masturbating?"

"Not yet, I'm trying to find the O. Building."

"Where is the Old Building?" she misunderstood me.

"No, the O. Building."

"It's probably the old Whitlock offices over on Wall Street."
She gave me an exact address.

I thanked her, told her I was masturbating, and hung up.

FACT: I WAS MYSTERIOUSLY BORN IN TOKYO
WHILE WHITLOCK WAS THERE. AND THEN MYSTERI-
OUSLY PUT UP FOR ADOPTION.

FACT: I WAS MYSTERIOUSLY GIVEN A WHITLOCK
SCHOLARSHIP EVEN THOUGH I NEVER APPLIED FOR
IT.

FACT: THE GRANT WAS SUDDENLY CUT AT MY
TWENTY-THIRD BIRTHDAY.

FACT: MY ADOPTIVE FATHER WAS NEVER VERY
PATERNAL.

QUESTION: WHY WOULD AMY, A JUNIOR PARTNER
AT ONE OF THE COUNTRY'S BIGGEST LAW FIRMS,
NEED TO MOVE IN WITH A NUTCASE LIKE ME?

All roads pointed to one answer: **?**

Early Tuesday evening, I dressed in office formals, an old
tweed suit. As I was about to leave, I decided not to take the
cheap handgun. I carefully slipped it under my pillow as any
good member of the NRA would.

I took a city bus through the constipated bowels of lower
Manhattan. I arrived at a filthy, old, limestone office building
on Wall Street. Under the tarnished plaque it read, WHIT-
LOCK INC. Long before the sudden and erratic growth of the
American economy, rising like the bow of a great ship, reaching its greatest heights just before it majestically slips under,
before the freakish erection of rhombus-shaped buildings and
the picket fences of adjacent skyscrapers that rendered this
neighborhood into a slow-motion parking lot of traffic at the
base of a human-filled air shaft, before all that, this modest
monstrosity must have been one of the first office buildings in
the area.

Six o'clock on Tuesday, an hour before Amy's fateful TOB
meeting, I purchased a weekly leftist newspaper and sta-

tioned myself across the street from the old building. I ate a tuna fish on challah while waiting for Amy to show up. I stooped behind and around structures, compelling the too-tight belt of my too-loose pants to dig painfully. I unbuckled it and waited. Slowly, strange sights appeared. Unusual men emerged. And they didn't arrive in any of those tacky rec-room-on-wheels limos either. These guys came in chauffeur-driven Rolls or classy, old, English sports cars, which they illegally parked out front, fuck the parking ticket.

In some cases, they got out of private cars. Who were they? There were about a dozen in all, usually with at least one bodyguard as an escort. They were all white, older men, well-dressed with strange clothes, costumes of aristocracy, gold-capped walking sticks, monocles on small vest chains. In one overdone case, a Prussian-looking riding crop tucked under an armpit; in another case, right out of central casting, an antique wicker wheelchair: Old money smelled of geriatric urine. My belt slipped off my pants.

From out of nowhere, a bouncy rottweiler walked up the street and looked at me angrily as it passed, then squatted and took a steaming dump before proceeding on. Along with pit bulls and dobermans, rottweilers are the turnstile jumpers of the pooper-scooper laws. Before the commanding canine could bounce away, a cop car paused.

"Hey," a rottweiler in a cop uniform called to me. "Clean that up." He pointed to the poop.

"He ain't mine," I said plainly.

"Clean it up or I'll give you a ticket."

"He ain't mine. Give the dog a ticket." The cop got out of the car, halting traffic all the way back to Brooklyn.

"What, do you just carry a leash on you for kicks?" he said, spotting the leather belt in my hand.

"This is my belt." I held it up.

"What are you doing here? Let's see some ID." Letting out a sigh of protest, I unfolded the copy of the *Village Voice* I was planning to get disgusted by, and shoveled up the expelled remains of the rottweiler's last victim. Deputy Dog passed, and I resumed my wait.

As I grew hypothermic in my hot-and-cold guessing-game of hunches, Amy's cab screeched to a halt before me. As she appeared, and the driver tore off her deductible metered receipt, I felt the tender scab of healing love rip open. "Amy, I love you," I muttered to a mailbox that doubled as a conduit for my heart's thwarting.

Not knowing what else to do, I figured that I should try to break into this odd little gathering and confirm once and for all that paranoia was not the central governing force in my life. Something was up. I had to go upstairs and find out what role these senior citizens played in my life. The old building had a main entrance and a large, metal set of janitor's doors. I tried the janitor's doors, yanking and pulling, struggling and wheezing. Then I went around to the main entrance. A near-dead security guard dozed before a dozen closed-circuit TVs and switches. I passed him and his seismographic snoring, and snuck into the only elevator in the bank that was still functioning. The button panel required key-access to each floor. Fortunately, the tumblers to one floor were switched to open. I pushed the button for that floor. Loud mechanical sounds from above must have heralded my coming.

CHAPTER THIRTEEN

FROM 'HOW'M I DOIN'?' TO 'GIULIANI TIME' AND BACK AGAIN

It is both a reality and a bad dream, but its deepest reality lies, strangely enough, in its manifestation as a dream," wise man George Kennan once said about another nightmare.

When the elevator door opened, I stepped into the dreamscape of a large, empty, unlit floor. Distant lights at the far end of the room illuminated a table. People were seated around it. As I approached my heart started fibrillating. I recognized Amy, the only kitten among a bunch of old toms. She saw me before I could reach the table.

"I've pieced things together," I confessed.

An elderly man leaning on a golden, lion-headed cane rose from his chair and began a presentation in a strange accent: "The Whitlock Corporation was founded in England in the mid-eighteenth century, 1752 to be exact. Slowly, in the late-nineteenth century, it invested more and more in America. Finally it was rechartered here in New York. Now, economic domination has slowly been revolving eastward. Young man, this is not some petty frat prank. We don't deal in vengeance."

"Since the late-'60s," a guy with a Van Dyke beard took the ball, "the Whitlock Corporation has made heavy investments in the Japanese economic infrastructure. Now the principal

179

problem, as you must know, is that there have been many restrictions forbidding foreign investors in Japan, especially back then."

"So?" I asked him. All eyes looked to one man who had been sitting in darkness the entire time. He suddenly flipped on a lamp. I walked over in disbelief and touched his face to see if he was real.

"Mr. Ngm, what are you doing here?"

"Am I not your father? Can't you address me as such?"

"I'm sorry, Mr. Ngm, it's just that…"

"The Japanese government," he began, "was particularly worried about the future holders of this stock."

"But what do you have to do with all this?"

"You must understand," interjected the Van Dyke beard, "this money is locked in Japan. They won't let us take it out. All we can really do with it is reinvest it and wait."

"I am a member of this board," Mr. Ngm replied.

"This isn't going to end with a lion and a chicken is it? I know that story."

"Whitlock is on his way here. He should be the one…"

"He's my father, isn't he?" I asked Mr. Ngm.

The group of men looked at each other strangely and silently. Finally Ngm spoke: "A secret clause was built into the 1962 trade agreement between the Japanese government and the CEO of Whitlock Inc. It stated that among Whitlock's trustees, he had to accept a Japanese citizen. That's when I was voted a member of the board."

"What does all this mean?"

"The agreement also stated that a future trustee with quite a few powers would come to the board on his twenty-first birthday." I was twenty-three, so I couldn't be the Anti-Christ.

"Am I on *Candid Camera*?"

"The board of trustees, as you can imagine, crosses a lot of borders. National feelings at times run deep. We have an ex–U.S. president and a former prime minister on our board.

"So Whitlock, to appease many of the Americans on the board, agreed to have his son born in Japan and thereby be a citizen, but he counter-stipulated that you must be raised here..."

"*America's Wackiest Videos?*"

"I assure you we did everything for a reason. The result was that you were from the sperm of Whitlock."

"Am I going to be a patsy for some assassination?"

"I have a meeting in Geneva at 3:00 and no time left for this *Oliver Twist* crap," said the dick with the Van Dyke beard.

"Mr. Ngm very graciously gave us permission on behalf of the Japanese government to delay your awakening," the double-headed cane said.

"We were trying to let you grow up a bit more," said the Van Dyke dick. "After all, we're not insensitive. It must be somewhat traumatic to learn that you were manufactured as a stipulation, a voucher to a corporate agreement."

"You're not being entirely honest," a new bow-tied figure added, staring at a distant figure behind him. Turning around, I could see him through the smoke and shadows. Whitlock had arrived.

"There was a force on this board," the double-headed eagle added, "that did not want you to assume your seat, who felt you were *mentis incompetence*."

"Incompetent!"

"This board decided that you had to pass a series of character tests," Whitlock explained.

"Tests?" I asked.

"Character assessment tests," said the double-headed cane. "We wanted to see several things. Among them, we were curious if you would fight for Amy, and stay with her."

"We were also interested in seeing if you could handle wealth," Whitlock said. "That money I gave you was in fact the last test."

"The money? You mean the half-million?"

"How did you handle it? Anything that happens here will be incumbent upon its full return."

"I still got it. I mean, I spent a couple of hundred, but I can make it back."

"Return what you have. You can make up the rest later."

"Fine." A McDonald's binge, a tourist night in New York, donations on a subway, and the purchase of an illegal handgun up in Harlem couldn't have destroyed more than five hundred bucks. I could get that much back selling my collector's issues of *Screw Magazine*.

Whitlock vanished off to a distant room that I suspected was a toilet.

"How could you do this to me?" I asked Mr Ngm.

"If I told you the truth, it could have jeopardized your status on this board."

"I don't mean that!" I yelled back. What was the point of trying to explain what it was like never having a father? How could I articulate the lifelong ache of rootlessness? It was apparent that he felt uncomfortable. Besides, I had already reached overload. I rose and walked through the darkness of this empty void. Behind me I felt a perfumed presence— Amy.

"I can't believe this," I muttered. "This is unbelievable."

"That's why you were paranoid all your life," Amy replied, and quickly added, "It's also why you suffer from certain character ailments."

"What character ailments?"

"Low self-esteem, manifesting itself in your selfish and sleazy nature. You don't trust anyone."

Suddenly it all fit together; she was getting even. "Amy, I'm sorry about our night of love and pain, but I don't deserve this!"

"That wasn't me. We never had conjugal relations," she said.

"Deny if you must…"

"Remember that middle-aged lady in the waiting area?"

"What waiting area?"

"Of the optometrist's office."

"No."

"Well, there was one there. Didn't you wonder why I insisted you had to get an eye operation just as I was coincidentally coming down with laryngitis?"

"What about it?"

"That case of laryngitis left me completely mute two days ago, remember?"

"So?"

"Do I sound like I have laryngitis now!?" she hollered.

"No, but you could have gotten over it."

"You couldn't see me, and I didn't have to speak to you. A body-double made love to you."

"But why did Whitlock…"

"You're Whitlock!" she hollered.

"You're confusing him!" Whitlock yelled from across the sea of darkness. Members of the board were parting now; others roamed absently, perhaps senilely, around the darkened floor.

"My parents were a trade agreement," I reckoned aloud.

"You were not neglected," Amy interjected.

"Everyone in this room had some hand in your upbringing," said the Ngm trustee affectionately. "We all had real concern for you. We would meet on a regular basis and review your life to try and find ways to generate and funnel love to you."

"We reviewed video tapes of you," said another misshapen slab of humanity. "We tried to get the right meals into your body."

"Flintstone over here," the Van Dyke pointed to the bow tie, "worried about your sex life. He tried to engineer a romance. He gave you a choice of girls."

"What? When?"

"At a bar near Herald Square shortly after that phony-operation escapade," Flintstone replied. I guess no one had ever told him about the children's cartoon of the same name.

"You mean those three girls who weren't *Charlie's Angels?*"

"Yes, and you rejected all three."

"They were paid for?"

"Actually," Van Dyke snickered, "I commend the boy's instincts."

"Instincts?"

"In fact, you could resolve a small wager. How did you know they were all transvestites?"

"I refuse to believe this!" I yelled. "You're all a cartel of out-of-work actors."

"But I was your legal father, was I not?" Ngm approached.

"You ran a failing bonsai plant company."

"That was a front. You never saw where I really worked."

"Yes I did, I saw the warehouse—on Seventh Avenue."

"We rented that space just to substantiate the lie."

"Where's Mother?" I asked anxiously.

"There, I had some problems. It's difficult hiring a woman for a lifetime role. The woman who played your mother till the age of seven moved to Baltimore. The second lady who played your mother felt the entire idea of deceiving you was disgusting, and quit just as you reached puberty. The last person who played your mother died suddenly."

"Ma died?" I asked. I had liked the last mother most of all.

"No, actually, she quit. Her name was," he opened a note-book and checked a page, "Laura Burrell. She died shortly afterwards."

"Amy, I beg you, tell me how much Whitlock paid you to make you all do this."

"Not a cent, he didn't have to." There was a strange mix-ture of sadness and panic in those soft, moist eyes. Quietly she explained, "No one outside this room knows this, but my real name is Amy Whitlock. Dad and I...well, I am your older sister."

"But, but…I love you."

"I love you, too, brother." I should have recognized it before; it made complete sense. After all, all love is merely a narcissistic projection. It was inevitable that I would fall in love with her. What else was Amy but me in a dress? Admittedly, the operation had brought out the beauty that was hidden within me. As I reckoned with the thought that she was my sister, I tried to neutralize the sexual feelings I had, but it was confusing.

"You are a full trustee member of Whitlock Incorporated," Whitlock said. "Just sign some documents and then you can go."

"You'll be given an appropriate income, based on dividends, and a portfolio we've been keeping for you. Its worth is comparable to that of any other member, save my own, of course."

"Why the job as a refrigerator repairman?" I asked, still trying to tear holes in their conspiracy.

"You needed a livelihood," Ngm said.

"And you are hostile to corporate America. That's the great irony. We truly tried to prep you for a place here. Hell, we tried to prep you for the presidency of the company…"

"Right!" I whooped. "And Whitlock yanked me out of the graduate program."

"Yes," Whitlock replied, "because we discovered you were about to drop out. We were hoping to create a frustration, to renew your drive to finish school."

"How about Veronica, the Dean's secretary? Why'd you…"

"Oh, we had reason to suspect that she was a member of the MOSAD, so we had to disengage you. We bought her off."

"The MOSAD? The Israeli secret service, MOSAD?"

"If not them, then the Israeli lobby. We have reason to suspect they stumbled over the secret of your true identity while you were in Israel."

"That's insane!"

"Operation Turkish Delight was a strategy designed to

defeat the Armenian Memorial Day Bill introduced by Senator Bob Dole," Whitlock said. "I don't know who Veronica was with, but once I agreed to use my political clout to kill the bill, she entirely lost interest in you."

"The operations then! How about the corrective surgery?"

"There were no operations," Amy replied, repressing a smirk.

"What?"

"Since birth, you had this self-concept of being small and ugly."

"But look, the scars!" I showed her my wrist and ankles.

"Those are only scars. Your height hasn't changed, nothing really changed. You were given a facial and haircut."

"How about the weight loss?"

"The weight loss was due to the so-called rehabilitative workouts afterwards, and the special diet."

"We tried to make you healthy!" Whitlock appealed.

"Be real," Amy said. "Do you really think I would force you to have an operation, or, for that matter, that doctors would operate on a non-consenting patient? It disappointed me that you were so gullible to this whole scheme. I actually thought it was quite amateur."

"I found out about the Bismarck operations," I shot back.

"What Bismarck operations?" Amy asked.

"You're from Bismarck, deny it!"

"I am, so what?"

"I found out all about the operation to take nerds of the '70s and turn them into corporate execs of the '90s."

"That's insane," Whitlock replied, rolling his eyes.

"But the Merlin Corporation is doing a clean up there!"

"What do you know of Merlin?" Ngm looked to Whitlock.

"I know it's a division of Whitlock Incorporated," I replied. They looked nervously back and forth.

"Hey, if I'm a trustee, I'm entitled to know what's going on!"

"It's nothing, just a nuclear waste clean-up unit," Ngm said.

"Are all these fuck-ups just an accident?"

"What are you talking about?"

"Everything from Vietnam and the Savings and Loan bankruptcy to nuclear waste clean-up."

"What are you talking about?" Whitlock asked.

"He's a trustee," Ngm replied, "and he's also your son."

Whitlock sighed and said, "Government debacles are America's chief booming industry, son. Learn that first and foremost."

"It's essentially what we do here," Ngm replied.

"That's great," I said, admiring the stench of it. It had finally sunk in. After a lifetime of despising these people, these modern day destroyers of Rome, it turned out I wasn't just one of them, I was a general of the Visigoths.

"It's only a fraction of what we made with the Reagan deficit," muttered Whitlock to Ngm.

"What?" I asked.

"In the words of Augustine," said Ngm, "do not seek to know more than is appropriate." I didn't think it appropriate to reveal that I had heard that same quote on Jeopardy the night before.

"This is only the executive committee of the board of trustees. The full board is meeting next Monday at 10:00 a.m. to vote on several strategies regarding the President's new national health insurance proposal. Try to come on time and look sharp," Whitlock called.

"But Dad, you still have to finish the last detail of the test, remember?" said Amy.

"What's that?" I inquired.

"The return of the money."

"Oh, gee, it's late," Whitlock said, checking his costly wristwatch.

"Now Andrew, it's imperative that you see this thing to its end," said the holder of the double-headed eagle cane.

"We are very particular about the rules here," Ngm added.

"Very well, son. Let us seal the final bonds of this contract."

"So be it," said Amy.

A limo was waiting for us downstairs. Dad, sis, and I got in.

"Actually," I said, "this really does make complete sense."

"It does?" asked Dad.

"Sure, this is what was missing from my life all along. A strong, supportive father. We could be one of the great father-son teams in history, joining the ranks of Philip of Macedonia and Alexander the Great; William Frederick I and Frederick the Great."

"How come the fathers are never great?" he responded.

As we drove, Dad and Amy discussed details of my ascendancy to the throne. While they talked about where I should live, who my support team would consist of, and a possible news conference announcing my mighty elevation, tears started coming to my eyes. Amy must have noticed the watering, because she commented, "You know those blue pupils you've got? They're actually extra-fine, extra-soft contact filters. You can take them out."

"Contact filters?!" I replied aghast.

"I'm sorry, but I was terrified at the thought of being mauled by my own brother," she replied meekly.

"I'm ashamed of how I acted before."

"Actually, the sex surrogate said you were wonderful," Amy replied.

"Did she really?"

"She absolutely did."

"God, I feel almost ashamed when I think about it."

"Well, all is forgiven." At that point, I noticed Dad gritting his teeth while staring out the window.

"Any problemo, Pop?"

"It just disgusts me that you have to go back to that shit-hole another night. Ngm should have provided you with better living conditions. Amy, I want you to get Joe a room at the Waldorf tonight."

"Will do." She was on the phone immediately.

"Joe, after a lifetime of stress and strain, I have one question to ask you."

"Sure, go ahead."

"Are you happy?"

"Truth?"

"Truth, son."

"I'm still in disbelief. I just can't digest all this."

"Well I wish there was something I could do."

"Well there is," I replied.

"Just say it."

"Do you have any money on you?"

"Well, not much on me," he replied, and opening his wallet, he offered ten freshly minted twenty dollar bills. Taking them out, he asked, "What do you want to get?"

"Nothing." I took the money and flipped down the window.

"What are you doing, son?"

"Something I always wanted to be able to do," I replied, and as we slowed down at an intersection, I looked around for homeless, but could only spot middle-class swine.

"Hey!" I yelled out to the bourgeoisie, "Grovel, you pigs!" I tossed the money out the window. It swirled in about a million different directions, and they didn't seem to notice at first, but finally one noticed and then the next. Looking through the rear window as we headed north, I watched a crowd scrambling and scratching.

"Now I believe it," I replied. Whitlock's bloated and bloodless face was fixed in comic horror.

"Relax," I counselled.

"Well, anything for you, hon," Amy replied. "After a life of destitution, I would have done the same thing."

"Hey, I don't care about the cash," Whitlock replied. "If you want, you can take the suitcase of money we're getting and toss it off the top of the Empire State Building."

"I'd like that," I replied gleefully.

"Fine, we'll do it," he ratified.

The limo pulled up in front of my place, and out we zipped.

It was strange as I climbed the steps, six at a time, thinking, I left here a pauper and I'm returning a prince. My gal, or sis, and pal, or pop, were fast on my heels.

"Hurry, and let's get out of here. Go somewhere and celebrate," Dad said.

Racing into the bathroom, I pushed the toilet aside to reveal the sacred hiding place. As I pulled out the cash-filled briefcase, I noticed Sis and Pop standing in the bathroom doorway, staring at me.

"So it was here all along," Dad said.

"Yeah," I replied.

"God, we searched the place looking for it. Who would have thought of a movable toilet?"

"Yeah, well. Here is most of it," I replied. "Let's go hurl it off the observation deck of the Empire State Building." Grabbing the suitcase, Pop punched me in the solar plexus. I went down hard.

"Sorry, my friend, this is where it all ends."

"Ba…da…da…"

"Don't be absurd, you little shit." Whitlock hit me again, a chop to my neck. I heard something inside snap like a rubber band.

"All right, we got the money. Let's get out of here," Amy appealed to him.

"No, after what he did to you, I want *you* to hit him, too!" Whitlock barked, and grabbing both arms behind my back, he shoved my head forward, a punching bag for free slaps.

"I'm not hitting anyone."

"Sis! Pa! Wuh?"

Grabbing me by my hair, Whitlock pulled me up. When I tried to turn to take a swing at him, he tripped me backwards into a bunch of boxes.

"You promised you wouldn't hurt him," Amy pleaded.

When I struggled to my feet, he punched me in the face. He seemed to be holding some kind of tube in his fist to intensify the blow. When I collapsed backwards on my bed, I realized it was all a fraud. He wasn't my father, she wasn't my sister. Then I felt it: the cheap handgun under the pillow. When I pulled it out and pointed it at my pseudo-Dad, his face turned white.

"It isn't real," Whitlock uttered.

"Please, let's avoid that cliché. It's real, and I'll use it if I have to." Amy and Whitlock stared at me.

"Get on your fucking fascist knees," I commanded both of them.

"What are you going to do?" he asked.

My nose was bleeding. Many little things were shattered and in pain. I ached as I walked. I was penniless, title-less. And things made little sense.

"How did you get Ngm to participate?" I asked, bewildered.

"People will do anything for the right sum of money," Whitlock replied.

"That's not true. It's not what you think," Amy cried out.

"If you hurt me, I'll have you killed," Whitlock swore.

"Then I better kill you."

"If you kill me, there are people who have instructions to torture you for the rest of your natural life."

"I have nothing," I replied. "I had it all, then lost it in a matter of minutes. My life matters little."

"Let it all end here," Amy appealed. "Let us leave with the money, and you'll never see us again."

"I plan to kill him, and rape and kill you," I revealed, and added as an afterthought, "Maybe I should rape him, too. Then I'll leave you alone and never see you again."

"All right, just listen," Whitlock said, rising to his feet.

"STAY DOWN!" I screamed. He fell nervously to all fours and talked out of the side of his mouth. I walked over and put the nose of the pistol to the back of his skull. Leisurely, I cocked the trigger. "Pray!"

"Oh my God!" Whitlock started weeping. I saw that I was standing in a puddle of piss; the man had urinated on the floor. The man was worth in excess of a billion, and I had him on the floor in his own urine. Holding the power to end his life in my hand, I felt good. But I couldn't murder him. It wasn't a question of morality (killing certain people is moral), but I wasn't prepared to end my life there. As poor as I was and as rich as he was, I still wasn't prepared to make that trade. (Besides, at that moment I remembered that the gun didn't work.)

"Get the fuck out!" I yelled at him. He rose, thanked me, and scrambled out the door, curiously mumbling, "Keep the tramp."

"Out! It's all over now," I said to the tramp.

"Let me just explain what happened here," she replied nervously.

"I killed my father and raped my mother. Spare me the bullshit. Just leave."

"Fine, neither of us have anything to gain or lose. I just want you to know we did fuck that night. You were supposed to fuck the body double, but…"

"Bullshit."

"Whitlock planned all this long ago. He wanted to drag you along much further. He wanted to get deep inside your head. He had a screenplay writer working on this. Planting clues and stuff. He wanted to string you along for years."

"Bullshit."

"What he didn't anticipate was that he'd fall in love with me, and even more, he didn't anticipate that I'd fall for you."

"Bullshit."

"Hey, I don't give a shit. But all that despair he went through for me, that was real. And that night you and I fucked, that was real."

"More bullshit."

Without a word she unbuttoned her shirt and pulled down the upper part of her right bra cup. There it was, my rodent-tooth brand, the love-hickey I implanted in a passionate frenzy.

"Do you want me to tell you what else you did to me? Do

you want me to tell you why you repulsed me and why I'll never be interested in you anymore?"

"Sorry about that, I didn't mean to…"

"I liked you. I fell for you. And you took advantage of me."

"I didn't meant to, I just thought humiliation and pain were necessary parts of truly great lovemaking," I replied, slowly seduced into her crap.

"Bullshit," she replied. "Anyway, that body double told him that you fucked me instead, and he went nuts. That's when he paid to get me back. Then when he ransacked your place and couldn't find the cash, he realized he had to pull the plug on this early. He was planning to continue this delusional torture for years."

"He's worth billions!"

"He's worth millions, not billions. He lost a lot by the end of the '80s. Hell, he can't afford to just throw away a million. Besides, the rich are misers. Didn't you see his face when you threw his two hundred bucks out the window? He was prepared to jump out after it."

"How did he get to Veronica?"

"He didn't. She just got sick of you."

"How about Mr. Ngm?" He couldn't have gotten to him.

"He half-bribed and half-extorted him. Don't be hard on that poor guy. He was very worried about you. Whitlock really worked on him. He made him all these promises: he'd free your transcripts, not have you arrested for larceny, and so on."

"You better leave," I replied. "I can't bear hearing any more of this." When Amy started to leave, I spotted the briefcase of cash. "Hey, take that. He's just going to send his thugs to get it. You might as well give it to him."

Amy picked up the briefcase and was about to walk out the door when she stopped and put it down. Taking out her checkbook, she scribbled something. She handed me a check for ten thousand dollars.

"What's this?"

"That is some of what I made on this assignment. You have

my work number, you can call me if you have any further
problem with Whitlock."

"What are you, a private detective or something?"

"Hell no. In fact, you picked me on this one. You picked
everything."

"I picked what?!"

"When Whitlock saw you had a crush on me, he brought
me in on this. Then he developed a crush on me, then I went
for you, but now I'm back with him."

"More bullshit."

"We weren't supposed to screw. That's why you became
blind and I was mute, but things don't always turn out as
they're supposed to, do they? Anyway, you picked everything."

"What does that mean?"

"All the bullshit that this was built on was bullshit we
heard you say. Bullshit that we knew you'd have a weakness
for."

"What bullshit do I have a weakness for?"

"Like the tendency to believe in complex and ridiculous
conspiracies. Also, your belief that beneath all the iconoclas-
tic garnish, you are a chosen son, waiting for some powerful
person to pull you out of your rut in life. Do something with
yourself. No one's going to rescue you but you."

Without reply, I saw the only woman I ever loved take the
briefcase, which held the only thing I ever loved, and head
downstairs to join the only person and thing I ever truly
hated.

For a long time, I sat amongst the ruined and renovated,
and felt an incredible sense of loss. So I really did make it
with her; that was small consolation to losing possession of
the world.

Suddenly I heard someone scrambling up the stairs. I
feared the worst—Whitlock or one of his infernal agents
coming to extract final revenge. With broken-gun in hand, I
ducked behind the door. Mr. Ngm entered.

"Mr. Ngm, freeze!" I said, still regarding him more as an

enemy than a friend. Mr. Ngm ignored my command and grabbed me, giving me an angry shake.

"Are you insane!" he screamed.

"Fuck you!" I punched him in the face. He kicked and punched, and I kicked and punched back.

"You're an inscrutable idiot!" he yelled.

"You're a fucking cold-hearted reptile!" And on the insults flew, back and forth, as blows were exchanged.

When we were both exhausted, we each crawled away, like two fought-out alley cats just sitting, panting on the floor.

"How did you meet a madman like that?" Ngm finally asked.

"At least he wasn't dead inside like you."

"Look, I gave what I had."

"How the fuck could you do that? How could you play along with him?" We both went to the kitchen sink and washed and bandaged ourselves among the dirty dishes.

"This Whitlock man approached me quite suddenly and said that my son was in deep trouble. He said you stole a large sum of money from him. He said that his attorney was pursuing a warrant for your arrest. He implied that he was going to do something terrifying to you. I tried to call you, but your phone was disconnected. Your mother was worried sick."

"So she wasn't dead? She didn't get sick and wasn't replaced?"

"Of course not! In fact, I kept trying to say things that were deliberately outlandish so you would eventually see the ridiculousness of it all and come to your senses! But you didn't! You just kept believing that nonsense! How could you be so gullible?!"

"Everything you said was something I had doubts about."

"That explains it," he said."Whitlock gave me a list of ten lies that I was to repeat and play a role in."

"He did that?"

"We actually rehearsed it several times. He had a theatrical director, and I had an acting coach. They were unemployed, non-union actors."

"I can't hear this anymore. I'm getting vertigo."

"Joe, I had no idea that you felt that way about me. I mean, I thought the whole thing was so absurd that you would never believe it. Did I really raise such a susceptible child?"

"YOU DIDN'T RAISE ME! YOU TREATED ME LIKE A GODDAMNED PLANT."

"But I've treated plants very well. They've been the very center of my existence."

"You weren't a Dad! I never saw you!"

"I tried teaching you self-reliance!"

"Do I seem self-reliant? The very first memory I have was you and mom saying that you adopted me to fill a parenting urge. What the hell was I supposed to think? Who were my real parents?"

"I have the file at home."

"You what?!"

"They were a young couple from the midwest somewhere. They were killed in an auto accident."

"They were?!"

"You weren't in the vehicle," he explained.

"Why didn't you tell me this long ago?"

"You didn't ask. If you like, you can have the file. You can check it out."

"I believe you." I paused, letting it all sink in.

"Joe, what will you be doing now?" he finally asked.

"Piecing together my shattered life."

"I didn't know you…I had no idea you had lost your grant to graduate school. Would you like to finish your education?"

"Yes, absolutely."

"Well all you had to do was tell me. You're my only son, you know. A child's education is his parent's final responsibility."

"I appreciate that." And then I tried to explain my mindset of the moment: "After all the histories I read, I came to realize that fate picks a handful of men who guide and decide for all others. Tonight, for about twenty minutes or so, I really thought I was one of those men—Bane Whitlock. I really thought I was someone consequential, truly corrupt."

"Yes, and so you were rich for that short time, and that's a feeling few people can know, even under deception. It should carry some value, some wisdom." He started walking around Amy's half of the apartment.

"But…"

"This apartment is nice," he called from Amy's room, "but why did you only have it half-renovated? And how could you afford it?"

"Amy lived in there. It's a long story."

"Come on, let's go get a cup of coffee; you can tell me all about it." So we went to an all-night coffee shop, and I told him the whole enchillada, about how Whitlock cut my grant and how I ended up scaring the hell out of him; how we then became best buddies and later sworn enemies. I explained how I got work as a proofreader and met the high-strung Amy, who became my psycho roommate; the court battles that ensued; the faux enhancement operations; and finally, how I actually deduced I was Whitlock's lost son, something we both laughed at. I also told him how I first thought I had made love to Amy and then I thought I hadn't, and then I learned I did, but I still wasn't sure.

"A regular loverboy, aren't you?" he joked as the sun rose, and the waiter finally brought over the check. He paid it, I left the tip, and we stepped outside. We silently, tiredly meandered south down Lexington Avenue as the city slowly awoke before us.

"I'm truly sorry, Joe," Ngm said out of the blue.

"No big deal."

"I don't mean that; I mean I'm sorry for failing you as a father. The truth of the matter is, I lost faith in humans long ago. I suppose that's the reason I turned to flora."

"Don't worry about it," I replied, searching for a quick and unsentimental departure.

"Joey, can you come over for dinner tonight?" he asked in a woebegone tone.

"I'd like to," I replied in a devil-may-care manner. "But I really fell behind 'cause of Whitlock and all, and I really do have to catch up on my history tonight."

He got the message and nodded a bit, looking off. I started receding, like one of night's shadows.

"Did you know that in 1581," he called out, "Ivan the Terrible accidentally killed his son and spent the last of his days in severe depression." I could see his sadness rising like steam through his grating attempts at reconciliation.

It was olive branch time: "Well, if you put it that way, Mr. Ngm, what time's dinner?"

"I'm not the great Whitlock, but I'd be honored if you called me Dad."

I did so and offered the man a handshake. He grabbed me and gave me a hug. For a minute I panicked, but then I hugged him back. And, for the first time ever, he kissed me on the cheek. A desperately unoccupied cabby screeched to a halt, unsummoned, compelling us to unhug. Dad smiled, I nodded, and Dad got in.

From out of the rolled-down car window in the backseat, before the cabby could zoom madly away, he pondered aloud, "Maybe all this wasn't so bad, son."

And poof! Dad was....

"All I asked was 'Did you make love with her?'" interrupted the fiftyish-year-old scion I was explaining all this to some sixty years later.

"All I told you was the answer," I replied, scanning the cherry-wood paneling that lined his private library.

"No one could remember all those tiresome details. Your senility must have embellished." Although I was old, my memory was still Viagra-erect.

A butler had just entered and stood behind me, alongside two brutish bodyguards. The rich prick, who resembled someone I couldn't place, waved him forward. The servant handed him an envelope.

"What is that?" I asked.

As the rich prick read its contents, he enlightened, "The only reason I let you ramble on like that was to hold you here for the results of your blood test."

I recalled having a pin-prick of blood extracted from me hours earlier, when his two thugs snatched me off the street and brought me to this castle in Long Island.

Looking up from the document, he uttered, "You could have just said yes."

"Yes to what?" I asked.

"My father died forty years ago," he elucidated. "My mother was killed in a plane crash about thirty years ago."

"Who were they?"

"Amy and Andrew Whitlock. After she left you, she married my father." I would have thought this was a final twist of mind-fuckery, but it was true. I had read it in all the newspapers as it happened.

"What does this have to do with me?"

"About ten years ago, I learned that my presumed father had been left sterile due to a childhood bout of Mumps. I spent the last few years trying to figure out who my sperm provider was. I had corpses exhumed and gave work to teams of private investigators. Finally, while perusing the privately printed memoirs of Andrew Whitlock's manservant, Wylie

Mandrylle, I stumbled upon this sordid little tale of a negligible sub-subordinate—you." He held up the letter. "The DNA test confirms it—*Dad!*"

Never had the word been said with such haunting sarcasm. The rich prick truly resembled a healthy, younger me in an Amyish sort of way.

"I refuse to believe any of it!" I said automatically. "It's part of that one great lie!"

"What lie?"

"The lie that compelled two Republican House Speakers to resign for the same sin they were impeaching a president for in the old millenium. The lie which stretches like an invisible wall that separates the rich from the poor. The lie that the 'religious wrong' lord over the rest of this country until they get caught with their robes up and beg for forgiveness into TV cameras. The lie that the old Soviet Union..."

"What the hell are you rambling on about?" He pushed my pause button.

"The lie of propriety! The lie of sanctimony! The lie of hypocrisy!"

"This is more of your paronoid pablum that my mother tried to keep in check, isn't it? Think about it. Since you're old and penniless, and I am one of the world's wealthiest men, this mess only splatters upon me, you senile numbskull"— spoken like a true son.

The boy was absolutely right. My Alzheimerish rebuttal had gotten the best of me. Absorbing the wealth that surrounded us, I realized that being his father—even if it wasn't true—was a *good* thing.

He sighed the sigh of kings, and asked, "You finally got the great Whitlock back. How does it feel?"

I shrugged gleelessly; it was all another lifetime ago. But for a moment an old feeling struck. I was finally rich. My son, the unwitting chip off my unworthy block, had usurped the monster and now he was welcoming me up to the throne— the start of a new dynasty. Crappy, freebee meals at senior citizen centers with tattooed and pierced, geriatric rock and rollers—gone. Waiting in foul-smelling lines with other octo-genarian orphans for mediocre hospital services—done. All the discomforts of an impoverished old age were over.

"Sonny boy, what's mine is yours, and the opposite!" I said, trying to hug my heir.

"Let me ask you something, Papa: Did you ever finish your grad-school education?"

"Not in the traditional sense, but…"

"What exactly did you do with your long life, Dad?" The rich man, my son, my savior, was asking me to open my files.

"Proofreading, TV, fun stuff like that." I assumed that he wanted to spend some quality time together, hang out.

"So you did nothing with your life." Like so many, he moved to premature judgement.

"Well that depends on how…"

"Boys, take out the trash," he said to the two apes that brought me in hours earlier.

They lifted me silently, carried me out the door, and tossed me into the backseat of their luxury sedan. After a fidgety hour and a half in which I speculated upon bringing a back-ward paternity suit—an infanity suit?—the car slowed down. One large paw opened my door, the other shoved me out. I rolled to a stop as they sped off.

I staggered to my feet and inspected myself for injury. My frail and wrinkly body was like a shriveled penis that would never know another erection. Of all the pranks played on me, old age was the greatest. My muscles and bones had dehydrated. My flesh and mind had lost their grip and luster. Even my veins were squirming away like earthworms on a rainy day.

The toss left me scratched and bruised. Passing between abandoned brownstones and the skeletal remains of vandalized cars, I recalled the old days—*fin de millenial* New York. The quality of life, 100 percent-rented, Starbucks-on-every-corner city was all but gone.

We had bad neighborhoods again: turnstile jumpers, sidewalk drug dealers, hostile panhandlers, funky junkies, hectic ethnics of all shapes and sizes. People didn't even scoop the poop anymore, and porn theaters blistered like herpes sores around Times Square once again.

As I walked, my son's question echoed in my hairy ears: *What exactly did you do with your long life, Dad?* I had fought for an apartment no one would now want, and had stored in it a lot of multifarious memories. I didn't leave behind any sandcastles of money or art. But is it so wrong to just live life and enjoy it? Between fun and function why must we choose the latter?

What else had I done with my life? I had slipped a changeling into a gilded cradle. One of the great American dynasties of wealth and power was headed by my offspring. The boy looked just like me, and even if he held me in contempt and claimed to be Whitlock pedigree, he was my DNA. A fart by any other name smells as foul.

And now, long after solitude, after need, long after anguish, and finally love, there was still endurance. I entered my musty, rent-controlled apartment—half-dilapidated, half-renovated by Amy all those years ago—and locked the door behind me.

Other selections in the AKASHIC URBAN SURREAL series

A HISTORY OF THE AFRICAN-AMERICAN PEOPLE [PROPOSED] BY STROM THURMOND
As Told to Percival Everett & James Kincaid [a novel]

312 pages, a trade paperback original, $15.95, ISBN: 1-888451-57-2

"This is the funniest novel I've read in years! I had trouble reading it because I had to stop to laugh out loud so often. Among many other things, it's a treasure of satiric humor. Don't pass it up!"
—Clarence Major, author of *Configurations*

DON DIMAIO OF LA PLATA
by Robert Arellano

200 pages, a trade paperback original, $13.95, ISBN: 1-888451-51-3

"Fear and loathing with Don Quixote at your side! Herein another savage journey to the heart of the American dream— but with *sabor* and *saber latino.*"
—Ilan Stavans, author of *Spanglish: The Making of a New American Language*

BOY GENIUS by Yongsoo Park

232 pages, a trade paperback original, $14.95, ISBN: 1-888451-24-6

"*Boy Genius* is a modern-day *Candide* . . . Yongsoo Park's combination of popular culture, high ideals, comedy, and serious intent makes for a joyride of a read."
—*Education Digest*

"Superb writing!" —*Clamor Magazine*

Also available from Akashic Books

SUICIDE CASANOVA by Arthur Nersesian
370 pages, hardcover in videocassette case, $25.00, ISBN: 1-888451-30-0
"Sick, depraved, and heartbreaking—in other words, a great read, a great book. *Suicide Casanova* is erotic noir and Nersesian's hard-boiled prose comes at you like a jailhouse confession."
—Jonathan Ames, author of *The Extra Man*

ADIOS MUCHACHOS by Daniel Chavarría
Winner of a 2001 Edgar Award
245 pages, paperback, $13.95, ISBN: 1-888451-16-5
"Daniel Chavarría has long been recognized as one of Latin America's finest writers. Now he again proves why . . . [L]ed by Alicia, the loveliest bicycle whore in all Havana."
—Edgar Award-winning author William Heffernan

SOUTHLAND by Nina Revoyr
Nominated for an Edgar Award
348 pages, a trade paperback original, $15.95, ISBN: 1-888451-41-6
"*Southland* merges elements of literature and social history with the propulsive drive of a mystery, while evoking Southern California as a character, a key player in the tale. Such aesthetics have motivated other Southland writers, most notably Walter Mosley." —*Los Angeles Times*

These books are available at local bookstores.
They can also be purchased with a credit card online through www.akashicbooks.com.
To order by mail send a check or money order to:

AKASHIC BOOKS

PO Box 1456, New York, NY 10009
www.akashicbooks.com, Akashic7@aol.com

(Prices include shipping. Outside the U.S., add $8 to each book ordered.)

Arthur Nersesian is the author of six novels, including *Suicide Casanova, Chinese Takeout, Unlubricated,* and the cult classic bestseller *The Fuck-Up.* The former managing editor of the *Portable Lower East Side,* he currently lives in New York City.